# SPADEWORK FOR A PALACE

## STORYBOOK ND

CURATED BY GINI ALHADEFF

César Aira, *The Famous Magician*

Osamu Dazai, *Early Light*

Helen DeWitt, *The English Understand Wool*

László Krasznahorkai, *Spadework for a Palace*

Clarice Lispector, *The Woman Who Killed the Fish*

Yoko Tawada, *Three Streets*

## FORTHCOMING

Natalia Ginzburg, *The Road to the City*

Rachel Ingalls, *In the Act*

# SPADEWORK FOR A PALACE
## ENTERING THE MADNESS OF OTHERS

# LÁSZLÓ KRASZNAHORKAI

translated from the Hungarian
by John Batki

STORYBOOK ND

Originally published by Magveto in Hungarian as *Aprómunka egy palotáért* in 2018
Published by arrangement with Rogers, Coleridge & White, agents for László Krasznahorkai

AUTHOR'S NOTE: Grateful acknowledgments to the Dorothy and Lewis B. Cullman Center, James Wood, Francesco Pellizzi, Gini Alhadeff, Colm Tóibín, Peter Straus, Aleksandra Wagner, Barbara Epler, Forrest Gander, Aladár Sarbu, Gabriella Vöő, and David Bell

PUBLISHER'S NOTE: Grateful acknowledgment is made to the Estate of Lebbeus Woods for permission to quote his "By Way of Resistance," originally published in *Architectural Resistance: Contemporary Architects Face Schindler Today*, Peter Noever, ed., MAK Center for Art and Architecture and Hatje Cantz Publishers, Los Angeles, 2003, copyright © 2003, 2009, 2021, 2022 Estate of Lebbeus Woods

Manufactured in the United States of America
First published clothbound by New Directions in 2022

*Library of Congress Cataloging-in-Publication Data*
Names: Krasznahorkai, László, author. | Batki, John, translator.
Title: Spadework for a palace : entering the madness of others / László Krasznahorkai ; translated from the Hungarian by John Batki.
Other titles: Aprómunka egy palotáért. English
Description: First edition. | New York : New Directions Publishing, 2020. | Series: Storybook ND | Originally published by Magveto in Hungarian in 2018 as Aprómunka egy palotáért.
Identifiers: LCCN 2020012677 | ISBN 9780811228404 (hardcover) | ISBN 9780811228411 (ebook)
Classification: LCC PH3281.K8866 A6713 2020 | DDC 894/.51134—dc23
LC record available at https://lccn.loc.gov/2020012677

10 9 8 7 6 5 4 3 2 1

New Directions Books are published for James Laughlin
by New Directions Publishing Corporation
80 Eighth Avenue, NY 10011

# SPADEWORK FOR A PALACE

*Reality is no obstacle*

I am not related to their famous author, but all my life they've been bothering me about him, just because our names are so similar and thanks to one or two other trivial items, it's always the same thing, people love to discover so-called interconnections, they're always contriving them, so to hell with them, when they come across someone whose name is melvill their ears prick up, then the repulsive reporters arrive, followed by Columbia grad students with their troubled eyes, and yes, that's exactly what happened, they found me, they gave me deep and meaningful looks, claiming that it wasn't because of that, but yes it was, I knew, it was because of my name, only because of that, though you could have heard a pin drop when they learned that I too resided on East 26th Street, and that I, too—and this in fact was a true coincidence—that I, too, had worked for a while at the Customs Office, yes, they could point out that both he and I worked as customs officials, but so what, I worked there only for a little while, that has no significance whatsoever, and anyway I happen to be a librarian—I almost had myself saying a born librarian—who is simply accumulating notes about his connectedness with the Earth, to which they would reply, well, that that's no big deal, you know mr melvill, not to shock you, but we all have that same connection to the Earth, yes, dripping with sarcasm, that's how they'd amuse themselves, when I unfortunately happened to accidentally divulge something about this connectedness interest of mine, but as far as I was concerned they could make fun of me as much as they liked, they could laugh themselves sick, because, though I might have accidentally let drop a smidgen or two, I never really revealed to them the essential thing, namely, that *my* connectedness with the Earth was radically different from theirs, it was not just any old connection, but a *permanent* connectedness that I maintained /and STILL DO!!!/ with the Earth by which I mean that for some time now I have been constantly *conscious* of this connectedness, whereas they were merely babbling nonsense, unconscious of what they were saying, letting words flutter this way and that, without anything to back them up, and, trying to pounce upon one thing or another, these reporters and grad students were just spouting a flurry of empty words, to hell with them all, they were not in fact interested in anything, not even what they'd been assigned to report on, something they hoped they could dish out for their readers, or write up for a seminar presentation, or what they were pretending, *wow*, to be enthusiastic about, but no, I decided they were definitely not going to dish me out to anyone, nor would I be the subject of some seminar paper, I won't have any of that, that's what I told myself, resolving not to let them distract me, because besides fulfilling my duties at work I have been living only for these jottings (if I may, without any pompousness, put it that way) though without the least intention of publishing these notes at some future time, because even a librarian is entitled to have an obsession, no?, and in fact probably every librarian has some little foible, in addition to having to deal, like myself, with what's commonly called "flat feet," since almost all librarians have this problem, although I must point out here that in my case it is not actually "flat feet" but a case of abnormal bony architecture of the feet, which is *quite* something else, and if I have the patience for it I will later explain what my condition is, as it's not just flat feet, I repeat, but a lowering of the medial longitudinal arch, and moreover a librarian may be permitted to have some foibles as well, and in my case it's unequivocal how this began because once I am on a scent I persist in following it, that was how I picked up on Melville, at first for the obvious reason and only superficially, without getting very far, just getting acquainted with him, but then I took a closer look to find out who he really was as long as we had this proximity due to the shared name; well then, one time my wife—always a fiend for art openings—after much prodding persuaded me to go with her to MoMAPS1 where at a deadly boring exhibition I discovered some work that TOTALLY did not belong there, work by Lebbeus Woods, a name I had never heard before, since architecture, especially the architecture of New York City, of Manhattan, had never been my particular cup of tea, everyone always raves about the architecture of Manhattan, those in fact horrendous, oversized, hulking building-monsters thrusting into the sky, just monstrosities, actually, not even buildings, Golems, good God, Golems in these streets so tiny and narrow, it is a madhouse, really, I always thought so—and still do!!!—Manhattan is a nightmare come to life, dreamed up by evildoers on a rampage, yes, I am referring to that nightmare created by a malevolent fate, of everything ending up in the hands of the real estate people, the slimiest gang in the history of human scum, real estate people I was always convinced—and still am—wreck and spoil everything they touch, everything within their reach, and since everything *is* theirs or *will be* theirs, and since this is what's been going on all along and keeps on happening in Manhattan they have been wrecking the place nonstop, and they keep at it, what, you say there's not enough land?, well then, why don't we just build vertically, we can buy up the air above, or have we bought up the air rights already? great, keep going, higher and higher, that's how it's gone, in my opinion, which is of course of no interest to anyone, but that's how it is, I live here, not liking what Manhattan's become, not liking what Manhattan's turning into all the time, Manhattan's no "frail, solitary taper," was it Ted Hughes who wrote that, or maybe it was one of his Eastern European poet friends, a lot of that kind of stuff comes from that neck of the woods, it doesn't matter, I can't remember, the point is I have no soft spot for that kind of drippy romanticism, that's what it is, exactly that grotesque romanticizing of the vulgarity of Manhattan, for Manhattan, let's be clear, is vulgar, it's no frail taper, Manhattan is a quivering monster deliriously fetishizing money, Manhattan is the coarse, raw, aggressive, ostentatious, megalomaniac, greedy, oppressive, hypocritical empire ruled by that dreadful horde

of vicious real estate speculators, yes they've comman-
deered it all, I can say so a hundred times over, this is
where the most vicious gang in the whole world is found,
I am certain of that, even though I'm unable to prove
it, oh well, never mind, in any case, there loomed Lebbeus Woods, there in that exhibition where about a hundred or two hundred so-called artists displayed their
horrendously vapid nothings, the stuff amassed and
dumped there for that show could only create an almost
sacral NOWHERE, and not just the NOWHERE of
works which are sinfully bad, they couldn't even be
called that, they were simply one and all depressing
specimens of that dreadfully dreary striving to meet
expectations, MoMAPS1 made room only for the panicked camp followers of panicky trends who wanted just
one thing, that is, "to belong," no matter where they
came from, they craved only that, having about as much
brains as a raw pumpkin, for even those who might
have been capable of more chose to sidle along, to get in
line, to not miss out on the party, craving only "to belong," the only thing that mattered was "to belong," as
if "to belong" were the only possible road to existing as
an artist, as if being an artist was only attainable by
belonging, the cowardice was appalling, as if there were
only this one stick of gum that everyone had to chew in
this great "belonging" until the end of time and then
suddenly right there on the third floor, in the midst of
all this fluff, out of this great NOWHERE, here comes
this giant, this improbably named Lebbeus, what kind
of name is that, perhaps it's used only in the Midwest
where people still read the Bible and where it is taken

to mean something like "man of heart," if I remember right, but I'm not sure, it's worth looking up, and I will, but not right now, because my main point is that there he was on the third floor to demonstrate *what* art is, because even I know that art is not some enchanting quality that manifests in material or intellectual *objects*, no, none of that crap, if you'll pardon me, art is not something that resides in an *object*, art is not some aesthetic statement, not some kind of message, there is no message, and in any case art is merely related to beauty, it is not identical with it, and especially art does not limit itself to enchantment, no, in its own extraordinary way art even banishes that, so that it is not in a book, a sculpture, a painting, a dance or piece of music where we have to look for art, because we should not even have to look for it, since art is instantly apprehended, if it is present, so when we speak of art, enchantment is not the issue, but the fact that the presence of art creates, how shall I put it, an exceptional atmosphere within a given space, and this *may be brought about* by a book, a sculpture, a painting, a dance, a piece of music, even a person, that's the only way I can define it—art is a cloud that provides shade from the sweltering heat, or a flash of lightning that splits the sky, where, in that shade's shelter, or that lightning's flash, the world simply becomes not the same as before, a space is created that's suddenly very cold, or very hot—in other words, due to some ineffable agency, every single particle of a given space all at once becomes something *other* than its surroundings, but enough of that, I think it's not up to a humble little librarian such as myself to try to define art, and here I am not saying humble little librarian because I secretly have a problem with being that, I don't have a problem with it, I am not frustrated, I never was, I am merely stating the fact clearly, which is why I say, and will keep on saying, I am indeed a gray little librarian, that's right, and am well aware that I look it, too, and dress accordingly, neither tall nor short, fat nor skinny, but frequently wearing my gray suit, or else my favorite, my brown suit, I alternate these two, my gray suit and my brown, and what am I supposed to say, that this isn't so?, when that's how it is, and I know it doesn't make me special, neither do I intend to be special, I never did, I am exactly where I want to be, a librarian in a library, one who (picking up where I'd left off) has always had difficulties finding the apt expression, yes indeed, to begin to write something, to start composing, is torture for me, so how did I start this notebook?—the less said the better—I began it, crossed it out once, began it again, tore those pages out as well, and then, after I started throwing away entire notebooks, I grew utterly exhausted with starting anew, and simply dropped the whole thing, until I just ... well, I began all over again, and I know it's no great shakes to begin something with "I am not related to their famous author, but all my life they've been bothering me about him, just because our names are so similar, and thanks to one or two other trivial items," but it's always been like that with me, I was always lousy at expressing myself, I never had the knack of *diving into* the subject and of capturing attention with a flourish, probably because one, I am basically an idiot when it comes to writing, and because two, what I want to tell here has never been told by anyone before, and this makes it very difficult to speak, and on top of that I am not even really speaking, except this is the only way I can manage at all, as if I were speaking, sort of like a monologue, otherwise it's no go, this is the only way I can get down what I want to write, acting as if I were saying it to someone, whereas of course I'm not actually speaking to anyone, well, no matter, I just wonder, what could I have been thinking when I began this whole thing?— even now I still doubt that anyone could be interested, in fact no one will read this, I wouldn't want to impose that on anyone, nor will I get myself in a situation where anyone could have access to it, no, no one should lay hands on it, and here it's enough if I follow the secretive way of librarians everywhere, which was indeed my method back when my story began: we hide objects away from unauthorized eyes, meaning that I make use of all possible means to prevent an encounter, in other words, I do what my colleagues in the library and I had been trying to do all along, which was to prevent library users from encountering the books they asked for—it is quite another matter that generally reader and book still manage to meet, there wasn't much we could do to prevent that, but whatever little there was in our power to do we did—and I believe I can say, speaking on behalf of every librarian in the world who has fallen arches, we do not especially relish readers, to put it mildly, no, we do not relish them, the reason being, in my case and also that of many others, simply the abnormal bony architecture of our arches, as I had mentioned earlier, or in the case of yet other librarians, varicose veins, spinal misalignments, bunions, pelvic malformations, arthritic joints, things of that sort, in any case, suffice it to say that having to stay on your feet for hours at a time, or in other words all the time, ought to be reason enough for anyone, even if you happen to be a librarian, to feel irritable, don't you think?, although in my case, it isn't flat feet, I repeat, it is something quite different, mustn't confuse the two, I've had a severe case of over-pronation of the arch since I was a child, but in any event, in brief, our feet hurt, and *that's why*—I'm not above making a small joke that this is the *sole* cause, but of course it isn't, there are other reasons as well— we most definitely do not relish handing out books to readers, and it's no exaggeration if I now say that my story actually began with that nonrelish, because it's here, at this exact point, that I conceived the Grand Notion that if we could have had our way, we'd drive them out of the libraries, just as you drive swine from a jewelry store, though in fact jewelry stores are way too full of them, and you may take that literally, as I'll explain later, the point is that we would prefer to never allow anyone near our books, our books should remain in their places, as in our reveries, in their proper order, so that, I'd continue to fantasize, we might establish a Serene Paradise of Knowledge, or more accurately not of Knowledge but of everything *that has to do with*

Knowledge, things that librarians, granted, did not create, but we would be preserving, this is still the dream I am speaking of, and yes, on the one hand there would be readers who each day will try to enter the libraries in order to request books (to read them in situ or to take them out on loan) but they would not be able to come in and remove books from the shelves or outright borrow them, for the libraries on the other hand would be closed, yes my God CLOSED, permanently, oh, dear God in heaven, the books unmolested and unread, what a lovely notion even just to dream about, and here I will go one step further because, speaking for myself, I trace this vision back to around three months after I started working at the library, yes, by then I already had the feeling that this library belonged to me, and in fact I'd never been crazy about lending things—for instance, on days when they came around for the blood drive I never signed up, no, and what's more, if a colleague knocked on my door to ask for a pinch of salt, I had no salt to give away—much less a book from the library—I considered the library books to be mine the same way as my blood and salt were, that's how I felt after not even three months on the job, and that's how it's been ever since, I can't explain how I came to this realization so rapidly, but already back then, after three months, I felt as if I were part of some apocryphal story from the Bible, where the librarian is not some lackey at the beck and call of library patrons, searching out and handing over books, but rather a ... a ... a ... keeper ... the keeper of the Library, who stands fast in front of the

unmarked and undivinable entrance, a portal that cannot be entered, refusing to let anyone come in or to allow anything to go out, no reader may enter and no
book may leave the premises, that was my dream—conceived and growing and taking shape within me—the
secret dream of every librarian, although many would
deny it: go and see for yourself (and again I am not
speaking to any one in particular, as I've already mentioned I can only write if I address "someone"), yes, go
see for yourself, all librarians are like this, when you, a
reader, request something from them, the librarians
(and I mean the real librarians) will rarely look you in
the eye, and they are always irritable, they mumble
when you speak to them, without giving you an answer,
as if you hadn't spoken loudly enough, as if they'd had
trouble hearing your question, or as if they'd found
your inquiry simpleminded, and I could go on here, because that's exactly how I too have behaved, and as I've
mentioned, I never felt I was the only one, no, I had an
entire army of librarians standing behind me, and van-
ishing—their shoes squeaking off through the stacks—
at the sight of a customer approaching with a request
slip, no, no, and no again, we did not relish readers and
still do not, for in our eyes there is and there can be no
difference between one reader and the next, all readers
are alike, they interrupt, they impede and prevent us
from being real librarians, and, after all, a librarian, as
I've said, is not a lackey, such an idea implies an absolute misunderstanding of a library's role, yes, I began
to have a clearer and clearer sense of the situation,

especially mine, here at the New York Public Library, public library my eye, whoever came up with that appellation got it wrong, divorcing the concept of the library from its rightful definition and reducing it to designate a mere common shop, a lend-ing in-sti-tution, whereas libraries are towers filled with books—and here the "tower" is just as important as "books"—they are towers that ought to be kept permanently locked, and this notion became firmly entrenched in my mind as the months and years and, yes, decades went by, libraries (as I had written down already back then, when I was barely past my earliest jottings relating to the Earth), libraries (as I wrote near the end of my first notebook) are the most exceptional and exalted works of art, yes, that's it, and people on the outside should be gratified to behold them from a distance and reflect, *Ah, there is the library and I am here*, which is vastly preferable to Ah, here's the library, as they close in on it, which is of course far worse, but in any case, the ideal library with, say, fifty million books shall sit there, a treasure trove that no one should ever be allowed to touch, since it preserves its value precisely by virtue of standing by, ever ready to manifest this value, by being ready and sitting there, in other words, that's all, and after a time this was what I kept writing down day after day, and it became increasingly obvious that this idea simply could not be bottled up although—at this point!!!—I am not sure if anyone beside myself is able to appreciate such sanctity, but in any case I kept writing this vision down, unfurling the thought day after day, week after week, month after month, and with in-creasing clarity, as I wondered, did anybody still remember the old Croton Reservoir that had formerly stood here?!, why didn't they keep building?! higher and higher?!—and it felt good to think about this, and even if they haven't consciously realized it, every librarian must have had this thought at least once a day, especially at the lending services desk, where I worked, but enough of that ... and here I am at a loss how to resume, I've let myself get carried away a bit, I know, and probably will yet again ... but never mind, I've lost the thread, I'm getting old, I've been working at the NYPL for forty-one years, no wonder that I often lose the thread, now I can't remember what I'd meant to say, oh well, let's return to Lebbeus Woods, yes, Woods, a true visionary, that's what I loved about him right away at that much hullabaloo'd MoMAPS1 *landmark exhibition*, titled "Greater New York," where he stood out as a visionary, suddenly here was an artist, yes there among all those craven middle-class boys and girls so desperate for success, just a bunch of entertainment-in-dustry workers, I found Woods astonishing, as I told my wife at the time, take a look at this, here is an artist, look, and I pointed at a drawing depicting a gigantic something the moment before it crumbled to pieces, but still in one piece, an immense behemoth, a gravity-de-fying, colossal, wonderful, scary monstrosity resembling a vast, undefinable yet somehow insect-like machine rising over the harbor, from some waterfront space, flaring upward over the piers in a sudden panicked arc with its tip, like some beak, curving downward, it resembled nothing I'd ever seen, nor has anyone to my knowledge ever imagined anything like it before, no, no one beside this Woods could have dreamed such a thing up, the way it rose, overarching terrestrial space only to dive back down from on high, yes, just like a beak, or a talon, and yet remain hovering midair like some colossus with its immeasurable mass frozen above that space, acknowledging terror and destruction, but, as if terrified by something down below, to hover up above this space that evoked a shoreline—the viewer had the sense of a body of water, the sea, the ocean—I don't know how to describe it, and it is impossible to describe what I felt, when I suddenly realized that this whole thing was a *building in the process of collapsing*, and Woods had *actually managed* to capture that moment, that *penultimate* fraction of a second before disintegration, as this structure, astounding as it was—its surface already shivered into small pieces, but the whole thing still in one piece, still in its entirety—plunges downward (and as I later learned he made use of a color photo of San Francisco Bay, on which he drew the whole thing, so that the view opens up from the near shore of the bay), and we behold this shattering structure toppling on to the opposite shore with its inconceivable, incomprehensible pieces that are in fact facets set at extremely disturbing angles to each other, yes, it is about to crash down into the water, and it's no longer a building, but a being, a distressed being, tumbling down in our direction, almost down upon us viewing it from this nether shoreline, or perhaps I am greatly mistaken, and the fact is that every building is a distressed being of this sort, only that its distress, and the reality that it is a being, isn't apparent because we are blind to it, and me, I am especially blind, I don't know, well, in any case, I pointed it out to my wife, see, this is art, by which I meant that this exhibition space held art, as I swept my arm around the room that contained mostly Woods, this is *serious stuff*, Let's go home, said my wife taking me by the arm, because she frowned upon my babbling away like that, she being a true exhibition freak who went there not for the paintings and sculpture but because of the new silk jumpsuit that she had just recently acquired at Century 21, in other words, she was there truly for an exhibition, that is, her chance to exhibit her black silk jumpsuit to the artwork, the visitors, and the walls, since when she happened to have a newly acquired black silk jumpsuit she was capable of, how shall I say, ecstatic transports over a new show opening somewhere, but now she took me by the arm and dragged me toward the exit, well aware that I was getting all worked up and ready with a sweep of my arm at all the junk there to launch into a real tirade, who were these people and why did they amass all this trash when they had a Woods here, and what seemed especially outrageous to me at this memorable MoMAPS1 show was the fact that they had DARED TO DUMP all that stuff next to Woods, that they had been incapable of differentiating between such garbage and Woods, this totally flabbergasted me, and my wife could see that she wasn't going to escape a tirade, now that I had stumbled upon the polar opposite of all that I despised, seeing the works of this Woods, who, truth to tell, I'd never heard of until then, having never paid much attention to architecture, as a matter of fact, I had been paying attention only to ideas, ideals and philosophies, never personages, and most certainly not in any intensive way, the one exception being Melville, and in his case at first only because of the name, otherwise I'd had little interest in him, although eventually my involvement became all-consuming, having to find out what this man was like, someone who went by the same name as me, though of course the retort to that is, no, it is you who goes by the same name as his, but it's not worth arguing about, and one thing is certain regardless, and that is that it was more bothersome for me than it would have been for him, because, being an absolute nobody, I felt constantly obliged to launch into explanations concerning my status as a nonentity, which is no hypocritical belittlement of myself, if need be I will repeat this any number of times, I am nobody special, particularly compared to Melville, in other words I am just a little old gray librarian who, granted, on occasion wears brown, and here once again, if you will recall my suits, I am making a small joke, well, anyway, I am just a librarian named herman melvill, with problematic fallen arches, who has been dreaming for forty-one years about once, just once, not handing over to a library patron the particular volume that has been requested, and thereby taking the first step toward building what he—together with the rest of his colleagues who hide their true aspirations—*desires*, laying the foundation of a library in the true sense of the word, in this manner, taking a first step in that direction, that is, the proper direction toward building something that I would then be able to lay at the feet of a true genius, as I had begun to believe he was by then, and even all, though this wasn't much, hardly anything in fact, and although at first this Melville, I will admit, did not produce such an overwhelming effect on me, of course I remember *Moby-Dick*, with "Call me Ishmael" and all that, but I can't claim that I'd ever thought it had much to do with me, on the contrary, it had been a constant annoyance, back in school, on the playground, and then at my workplaces, the way they always came after me, saying "what's up with your whale, herman, why didn't you bring him along," that sort of thing, and the fact is that it wasn't so much his books that I began to look into, because at just about this time I had discovered my ongoing connectedness to the Earth, in other words it wasn't so much *Moby-Dick*, or *Billy Budd* or *Redburn*, leading to what this was all about, my being herman and melvill as well, but rather the life story of his biographies, and there I found something that aroused my curiosity, which was that no matter how many thousands of facts I gathered from those biographies the one thing I could never find out was what this Melville was *like*, and that's quite a serious problem, wouldn't you say?, when you read all these biographies, and of course I had no problem finding the ones considered the most important, so that I soon found my way to the great Hershel Parker, and Delbanco, and Jay Leyda, compiler of the *Melville Log*, and Charles Olson, and Mumford, and so on and so forth, I found all sorts of things in them, but I never got to know what Melville was *like*, I found out that he was tall, close to six feet, and I know what his house at Arrowhead looked like, also the one on East 26th Street, I mean I knew exactly what the interiors were like at Arrowhead, and on 26th Street, yes, I became familiar with every square foot of each room, and with the place where he preferred to sit when he smoked his pipe, and what his daily schedule was like, those were the sorts of things that I wanted to know, hoping that in some minor detail of daily routine or everyday habit, I might come across a clue, a clue that would lead to the answer I'd been expecting to my question of what he was actually like, but no, the more details I'd amassed the less I knew about the man it was my good or bad luck to be linked with, and that's how it happened that he'd truly aroused my interest, but it had not been decided yet that I'd persist, though once again, I was following a scent, which was the very fact that so many biographers had tried without success (although I would not go as far as claiming they were all mediocre nitwits, the ones who had attempted the task, because Hershel Parker or Andrew Delbanco or Jay Leyda cannot exactly be called small fry or nitwits), these men had done their homework thoroughly before setting out to write their texts, and probably they themselves were unaware that they had not succeeded, so it's quite possible that, should the occasion arise, if I had a chance to talk to them (after all they were still alive), I'd explain that, in spite of all their years of meticulous research, and then the labor of writing, they hadn't succeeded in capturing Melville—Melville was not there—and they'd be truly surprised to hear that such, alas, was the situation, rather regrettable for them, but not for me, because for me it was precisely their failure that signaled there was something worthwhile here, in their failure I found the embers to kindle my fire for really looking into the matter, into why these outstanding scholars had not succeeded in capturing Melville, the essence of Melville's being, but then the years went by and it became obvious that, in their wake, I too would fail to get any closer, my investigations, too, would prove fruitless, and I could not comprehend why, what exactly was tying up this knot now boggling my mind, after all my anticipation, and all my expectations that Melville would materialize for me through his own writings, or through my many repeated attempts to approach him via countless monographs and biographies and correspondence volumes and memoirs ranging on so broad a scale from the objective all the way to the subjective and partial, but no, Melville himself never makes an appearance, even though his circumstances do, the facts are somehow there—the residences, the surroundings, the children, the ships, the travels, the books, their reception, the streets, Hawthorne, Lizzy and the Gansevoorts are all there—but the essence is missing, somehow that plainly palpable essence of who Melville was is simply not there, how should I explain what I mean, I am not good with words as I've mentioned, I can never find the right ones, and I am well aware that this "who was he, what was he" is itself not the real thing, but you see I had asked myself, would I be able to conjure him up, just for me, and I couldn't, that's what I mean by what was he like, and who was he, but never mind, I had hoped I would never be in the position of having to explain this to others, because that wouldn't work either, of that much I was certain, but no matter, I once again set out to search through, or rather among, the materials available to me, perhaps I could then come across something that would quickly show me the way, intuitively, but there are no short cuts, I soon realized, after working through the close to two thousand pages of Hershel Parker, and the near one thousand pages of Jay Leyda, and Delbanco's four hundred pages (in those days I called them the Parker Two Thousand and the Leyda One Thousand and the Delbanco Four Hundred, as if they'd been track and field events), not to mention countless other volumes written about Melville, but all in vain, I didn't ever find Melville in them, and again I'm just saying (and naturally I am not addressing anyone in particular) that that's all I wanted, you see, to find out if Melville was there and he wasn't, it was as if there'd been a party where everyone invited had already assembled and we're waiting for him, glancing at our watches and still no Melville, and we keep raising quizzical eyebrows as the hours go by, and shrugging our shoulders and checking our watches and gazing at the door, as if hoping against hope that it would at long last open and there he would stand, but then all at once everyone simultaneously realizes that *Melville will never be here*, what the hell, this is totally absurd, I thought back then, early in the game, and that's when I started to look into the routes that—already a failed author—he used when he commuted daily to the Customs House, walking out of his residence, and taking a horse-drawn omnibus down Broadway to 13th Street, and walking from there west to his "office," and yes, for the sake of veracity let us right away enclose that office in quotation marks, because in truth it was a shack that he walked to, six days a week for four dollars a day, to manage paperwork amid all the commotion, yes, and that "office" shack was located approximately on today's Bethune Street, though that doesn't really matter, since back in his time, as I found out, the entire customs district along the banks of the Hudson as well as down by the present-day Staten Island ferry terminal and all the lower Manhattan sides of the East River constituted one big chaotic turmoil, as Melville had himself described it several times, granted, it was mostly in connection with the magic attraction of water, of the sea, there it is right at the outset of *Moby-Dick*, out on the water, sailing ships and steamships, barques, brigs and schooners, and on the land longshoremen, sailors, carters, loafers, pickpockets, dogs and cats and wharf rats as well as, yes, even though he makes no mention of them, customs inspectors, such as Melville, alas, was himself bound to mention whenever asked what he did for a living, for close to twenty years, for four dollars a

day, and in any case, having decided to verify the route
he followed, one day I exited at the rear of the library
on 42nd Street, and from there proceeded to Grand
Central, where I took the number 6 train to 28th Street,
and from there went on foot to the Melville residence,
just as if, in other words, I had been going home, and so
I arrived at point zero, because this was zero, the beginning, the alpha of this longish narrative, the starting
point where I too set out on *my rambles*, that is to say,
from then on every week—not six days as he did but one
day a week—I set out from this alpha point in the direction of Broadway, where unlike Melville, who took a
horse-drawn omnibus, I walked all the way down to
13th Street, not a negligible stroll even for a Manhattanite, not to mention a Manhattanite with a severe
case of fallen arches, which I will eventually define more
accurately, because I can describe this overpronated
arch with precise medical terminology even if roused
from deepest sleep in the middle of the night, yes, I
would still be able to differentiate it from so called "flat
feet," which is all to say that it was an especially long
walk for me, but never did I hesitate about going
through with it once a week, all the way down Broadway to 13th Street, as I said, and from there, still pro-
ceeding on foot, as the original Melville had, by way of
Gansevoort Street to the bank of the Hudson, and then
down along the river a bit farther, although now and
again I did not take the turn at 13th Street but continued downtown on Broadway, to turn Hudsonward at
some other point, in sum, I *usually* turned at 13th

Street, but not *always* at 13th Street, in part because back then, I didn't know at first exactly where that Shack had stood, where Melville the customs inspector stamped his paperwork, but also in part simply out of curiosity, for along the way I kept encountering things that interested me, or to put it more accurately, things that sidetracked me, and led me off somewhere, although this isn't to say that anything diverted my thoughts away from Melville, no, not at all, just the contrary, it was my ruminations about Melville that occupied my thoughts, preventing me from noticing where I happened to be, so that every week, when I set out on my Melville ramble, as I referred to it in my thoughts, it was in fact Melville's fault when I lost my way at some odd corner down by the Hudson, as I was for some time still ignorant of the actual site of the Shack for his paperwork and I just roamed about, with my mind always occupied by some fresh notion concerning Melville, but these thoughts often got mixed up with reflections that evoked the drunkard Lowry, because, as I advanced in this peculiar story on the trail of Melville, once I happened to recall that Malcolm Lowry, too, had roamed this neighborhood in his *Lunar Caustic*, yes, I was certain he did, and with that Lowry too entered the picture, because in all my readings I had never encountered anyone as thoroughly obsessed with Melville as Lowry had been, so I poked around a bit in the library regarding this Lowry, finding surprisingly little in Day, in Bowker, in the Gabrial manuscript or in the correspondence, and whatever else I had plowed through in my great excitement, for I do not deny that I was excited when I had reached this point, that is, the point where, in addition to Lebbeus Woods, I could link this Englishman to Melville as well, because by that time I was convinced that such parallels could not be *entirely* written off as coincidences, or at the very least they could not be utterly meaningless, though maybe they shouldn't be called parallels so much as similarities, or overlaps, if not interconnections, and I knew that the sort of writing-off that I, along with so many others, am liable to accept, or would have, had I not managed to hang on to my sanity, as indeed I had, although—and yet again here comes another on-the-one-hand and on-the-other—on the one hand, although the subsequent discovery of the existence of this next interconnection did not in the least mean the loss of my sanity, on the other hand, and once again, although today I am not entirely certain that this sanity will still be with me tomorrow, I've no idea, and at this place where I happen to be now, one may never know, another problem being that as a matter of fact I don't really care, you see what could I really lose if I no longer possessed it, my sanity that is, since the only thing that I lost due to my preoccupation with Melville was my wife, since I didn't really have anything else left to lose, with my colleagues I'd always kept up a purely professional relationship, from entering the library in the morning until exiting it at the end of the workday, it was only my wife with whom I had maintained a personal relationship even after I'd immersed myself in my Melville research, at work for un-

derstandable reasons I'd kept in utmost secrecy what
my simple initial interest had burgeoned into, and so
she, my wife, was the last person who'd hung on for a
while, and then she too was gone, probably it became
too difficult for her to put up with a man with whom she
could never go out sporting her current black jumpsuit
in order to surrender herself to experience, as she liked
to put it, never out to an opening, never a performance
at the Metropolitan Opera, not even a small get-to-
gether on the Upper East Side, no, never, nothing, not
with me along, because I was such an impossible person, and I never really had any leg to stand on about
that, since even then I didn't have such a great opinion
of myself, and I still don't know, in other words, where
was I ... damn, again I've lost track of what I wanted to
say, oh yes, I'd become convinced that if these three
plotlines had gotten so tangled up it could not be an
accident, although at the time I wouldn't have supposed
that ultimately it would not be about Melville, or about
Woods, or about this monstrous but irresistible Englishman stinking of self-pity even more than of mescal or
tequila and who, between ourselves, truly tortured his
wives to death—yes, while at work on his own complete
self-annihilation, he enjoyed tormenting them—yes,
how shall I put it, out of the most absolute selfishness,
because on top of busily, systematically and ostenta-
tiously dismantling and ruining and destroying and
murdering the man he *could have been*, he also de-
manded to be dandled and loved as a child, whereas my
own case was quite different, in my own way I'd done

everything possible for my wife, even if my sudden transports along with their subsequent obsessive itches for research were of course not exactly designed to please a wife, and indeed they did not please my wife, though perhaps if I had evinced a keener appreciation of those black jumpsuits, if I'd given them more than just a passing glance or two, but I didn't think much of jumpsuits, hardly even noticed them, and more to the point, I'd no words of praise for them, because I was too preoccupied with Melville, or perhaps even before that, with something else that suddenly had enshrouded my mind, but that's how it goes, she's no longer with me, and it no longer matters now, because far more important things are happening, but I shouldn't run ahead of myself so much, because if I do, then this account I am at last determined to give will become totally jumbled, although I must admit I'd agonized for quite some time over whether I should write down any of this, should I do it, because to be truthful I really did not want to have anyone reading what I wrote, and today *it goes without saying* that I absolutely don't want it read, in fact now the essential thing is that no one should read it, in other words, as you must have guessed by now, and once again I am not addressing anyone in particular—after all there is no one left to address, as I have mentioned I no longer have even a wife—so obviously you must have guessed by now that here I am speaking as the keeper of the palace, that from here on everything is tilting in the direction of the Permanently Closed Library, and above all tilting toward that first Veritable Block on this botched island, the Only One I would still be capable of loving—in fact, I'd go as far as to say worshipping, in this city, in Manhattan, yes, I am speaking about the Ultimate Block without doors or windows, the Block that in the most strictly literal sense would enclose within itself the first real library, and toward which I would be taking a tiny initial step by depositing inside it these notebooks I have been and still am writing, just one small step and nothing more, but as I began to reflect after a while, it would be at the same time the greatest possible step for me, and that's when it became unequivocally clear to me that I would keep writing these notes and that they would be the very first writing expressly intended for a library that would never be open, whose materials could never be read by anyone, not that I am saying that any reader would want to read personal notes of this sort, instead of Dante and Shakespeare and Homer and Plato and Newton and Buddha and so forth, no-o-o, of course not, I too would much rather read Dante and Plato and Homer and so forth, since not even I attach any great significance—more precisely and in fact none whatsoever—to what I have so far written down, nor to what is to follow, except that this is all I am able to contribute, so I will still write it down, I am not sure if I'm being clear, but that's all I intend to say about this, and now, after all this back and forth, I'll resume, and return to the afternoon when I had first set out downtown on my Melville Ramble, heading for Gansevoort Street, though that makes it sound as if I've been meaning to here point out—lo and behold—some significant moment, but no, I couldn't claim then, and I can't claim now, any one particular day, or especially any particular hour, there simply wasn't any exceptional moment like that, I just set out, on the ramble, that is from 104 East 26th Street in the direction of Broadway, turning at 13th Street toward the river, on foot all the way, unlike the great Melville who took a horse-drawn omnibus, I walked in my favorite walking shoes equipped with orthotic arch supports, the lowercase melvill, without a clue about where Lowry had set out from, though according to *Lunar Caustic* he too must have been rambling somewhere around this neighborhood, if we are to suppose, and we do, that all of Lowry's writings are autobiographical then we might safely rely, as I did, on *Lunar Caustic* to imagine Lowry's perambulations here, which of course did not mean that I could literally extrapolate the route he followed, for Lowry's path even when he was sober was not easy to extrapolate, much less when he was drunk, so I only permitted myself the most cautious hypotheses, just makeshift guesswork about the route he'd followed in search of Melville, when, as it seems, after ten days he was discharged from the psychiatric ward of Bellevue Hospital by the East River (which incidentally happens to be in my neighborhood) and of course the Plantagenet in *Lunar Caustic* is Lowry himself, who else, though this Plantagenet was, I take it, of middling height and somewhat chubby, and quite bald in the front on both sides, almost like me, except that I am even shorter, and so on, but anyway, regarding Lowry, who was in fact tall and sturdy, with decidedly heart-throb-type looks, let this much suffice for now, for a start, that it was precisely on account of Lowry and Plantagenet that I first went in search of the building where Melville had resided during the last decades of his life, on East 26th Street, where I too coincidentally happen to live, as I have mentioned in speaking of Bellevue, except that my address is near Second Avenue, whereas his house, as indicated by its number, is near Park Avenue, and so Lowry, when they kicked him out of Bellevue as *Lunar Caustic* would have it though in real life it was Jan who brought him out after she learned he was there (where he of course proved to be untreatable), and as Lowry he went home with Jan, while as Plantagenet he went out on the town, heading first of all to the nearest tavern for a drink, then to a second tavern for a second drink, and so forth, but if we can believe him, he had in fact meant to find the house where Herman Melville had resided, but was unable, either as Plantagenet or as Lowry, to find the place, he had no luck, whereas I had no trouble at all, for I had found out the address—how did I do it? I won't tell you!—just kidding again—I simply walked down my street, East 26th Street, all the way to number 104, or rather to where I'd guessed 104 would be, and then I immediately discovered the historical marker on the right side of the entrance (or was it the left?), evidently not much effort had been expended to make it very conspicuous, but there it was, and I found it, I can't help but write this again and again, how easy it was to find, with a degree of difficulty approximately comparable to finding the Empire State Building on Fifth Avenue, well, all right, maybe slightly more difficult, but only slightly, because if you knew the address, it was a cinch, yes, once you have the address, that keeps you from going in circles, you are there in the blink of an eye, but that wasn't the case with Lowry, evidently he had marshaled an overabundant supply of energies to find the place, and one might say he'd overshot the mark or fumbled the ball, obviously he had a supercharged inner drive, and having read all the memoirs and correspondence referring to him, as well as *Under the Volcano* and *Lunar Caustic*, I had always imagined Lowry to be, how shall I say, guided by his inner lights, and that's why he'd moved about in that meandering way, taking unpredictable paths, always so lost you see, and vaguely suicidal, both previously and subsequently, but especially at that period between 1934 and 1936, when he resided in Manhattan together with his first wife Jan Gabrial, and therefore I followed Lowry's wavering footsteps by not following them at all, realizing after some reflection that he was always there where I happened to be walking, so because of Melville, and later because of Woods and Melville, this man Lowry was always by my side, I didn't have to look for him, not at all, whereas I had to look for the other two, Melville and Woods, while Lowry, whether I wanted him or not, was simply there, no need to look, from the word go he voluntarily accompanied me on these rambles that I commenced one day, I no longer recall the time of day, perhaps it was an afternoon, perhaps an evening, when I emerged from the rear exit of the Public Library on 42nd Street, and proceeded to the alpha point, and began these walks, once a week, although I wasn't at all methodical about it, for I believed that it wasn't a method I had to follow but Melville himself, and that would provide my method as it indeed did, Lowry was there in any case, and as for Woods, I thought that once I was down there by the Battery he would join us as well, for I took him to be another peripatetic genius, whether pacing about in a small room or in the great outdoors, out in the streets, that's how, according to my researches, geniuses of this type tend to behave, it makes no difference where they are, they must keep walking, advancing to a certain point and then back, and once again the same, endlessly, and I'd believed that Woods belonged to this type, and since Manhattan took up so much of his attention, he must have first of all perambulated the area where he lived and worked, that is Downtown, but this hypothesis, as I found out after a while, proved to be incorrect, because although it's true that of course he walked from point A to point B, from his apartment to Cooper Union, where he taught for about twenty years, or from Cooper Union to Third Avenue, to buy a certain kind of sketchbook (which, I'd found out, was a specific type manufactured by Michael Roger in New Jersey, one that fit in his jacket pocket) so that he had walked about in a triangle composed of the apartment, Cooper Union, and the art supply store on Third Avenue, and here I almost forgot to add what I consider to be most significant, that is, there he would walk from the apartment or from Cooper Union to certain taverns—when he had resided in TriBeCa it was a particular tavern in that neighborhood, and when he lived near Battery Park, or the Financial District, it was other neighborhood taverns, depending on where his apartment happened to be at the time, naturally he would start out from where he lived, but he never walked around aimlessly, and was in fact not at all the kind of peripatetic genius I'd taken him for, a man who might set out to stroll about in TriBeCa or Battery Park or the Financial District and just keep walking while everything happened inside him, in his head, or in his heart, but no, Woods, when he could not stay at home, generally went out with some specific destination in mind, and among all of these destinations, the one constant spot, not counting the occasional trip to the art supply store at 62 Third Avenue to buy the sketchbooks he kept in his right-hand jacket pocket, was a tavern, because regardless of what part of downtown he happened to be residing in, he preferred to frequent the same particular tavern, not necessarily one that was closest to his apartment, but the one that proved most *suitable* from a certain standpoint, and here it doesn't matter which taverns these were, it's not important, I'm not going to list them—even though I know each and every one, it was easy to get the information, I will jot them down when I have the time, and if I remember to, above all though the important thing is that in his life just about every item was variable except for one, that there always had to be a suitable tavern where he could sojourn between 3 and 5 p.m., not on the dot, but approximately, and that's all I had really wanted to ascertain, whether he had a permanent destination he frequented with a certain regularity, and yes he had, though he obviously visited other taverns with his wife or friends or students, he liked to do that, not to mention that he liked to have a drink at home as well, in fact it was at home that he really liked to drink, mostly champagne, but from my point of view only the 3 to 5 p.m. tavern sojourns are of real interest, for these were the occasions when he was *alone*, at that time of day the taverns are practically empty, a relatively quiet time, even the music is not as loud as it becomes later in the day, so he could take his seat, in this or that particular tavern, and to start, order a vodka, then pull out the Michael Roger sketchbook from the right pocket of his jacket, light up a Dunhill cigarette, which was his favorite brand till the end of his life, and, with his pen in hand, depart without taking a single step, reaching for his glass from time to time and never budging from that table, yet on the move, in his imagination, as they say, walking the streets of Manhattan, his mind working all the time, his thoughts ranging over structures, tensions, force fields, plane surfaces' relation to one another, undulations and torsions, and, traveling the streets of Manhattan in his mind, he must have instantly realized what he was walking over, crossing

39

Broadway, going down to the waterfront, at times even taking the Staten Island ferry as tourists do, to obtain a distant view of the tip of Manhattan, and once I had learned about his routine, it was not difficult for me to imagine that on these imaginary rambles of his Woods had in fact been constantly crossing or grazing the routes that formerly Melville, and subsequently Lowry, must have followed, and so it happened that after a while, maybe about a year after my first ramble, I was walking on these routes with the *certainty* that I was treading in the footsteps of Melville and Lowry and Woods, and I mean by that that today I could be certain that the Melville route I had established for myself was exactly the same route where Melville's and Lowry's and Woods's genius had been working away and my only task was to engrave by means of my passage on this route the traces of these three geniuses found pre- cisely in these places, a task I had taken on with the utmost seriousness, how shall I put it now, not as one presuming to compare himself to them, oh nothing like that, it was really something quite different, namely that by walking the route once a week I paid homage to Melville who—whatever we add of Lowry's frenzied ad- ulation and Woods's cogitations about Manhattan—was preoccupied solely with the universal, whenever he was able to tear himself away from mundane troubles, some- thing he proved to always be capable of doing sooner or later, and now I will try to explain what kind of homage I was then and am now referring to, and why I owe this homage to Melville and Lowry and Woods, and why in fact we all need to pay homage to them, an homage, let me immediately add, that is not aimed at Melville or Lowry or Woods as such, but is homage, or to use a better word, reverence, yes, that more exactly expresses what I mean, reverence, toward this trio, I almost wrote Trinity, of Melville, Lowry and Woods, who direct our attention (or anyone's who is sensitive) to our ties to the universal, namely,

WHERE WE ARE.

I'm not sure whether all this is now sufficiently clear.

That we are in Manhattan.

And that Manhattan lies on top of a rock.

And that this rock is a giant whose size, mass and weight bring about the most intricate interconnectedness between us and the monumental forces of nature.

And that the present-day and, I am sorry to have to write, the future prevailing situation in Manhattan hides this interconnectedness.

And that it is the architecture of Manhattan that hides it.

And that the architecture that took shape in modern cities hides our existing connectedness to the question of WHERE ARE WE.

But not only architecture: all art and science and philosophy in the modern metropolis hides it. And some metropolitan art and science and philosophy hides our connectedness precisely by attempting to point it out.

Yes, they all hide the very connectedness that is most vital for us. In fact, the only one that is vital for us.

And when that connectedness is hidden, we no longer have any idea of WHERE WE ARE.

We exist in an adulterated space, for instance here in Manhattan, and—as in any other metropolis—and architecture is first and foremost responsible for this. As well as the arts and sciences and philosophies.

But architecture first and foremost. Then all the others, first and foremost.

My god, where must I begin, to make this clear.

Melville's connectedness with the universe was *constant*, meaning, at least as I understood matters, when, after reading all of his main works from *Moby-Dick* to *Clarel* as well as all the literature about him, and after not finding his person, I literally began to walk in his tracks, and these rambles made me realize in a flash that he was simply *unwilling* to engage at any other level than what we may call the universal—as long as I am connected to the universal, he said, why on earth should I be concerned with anything else?!: this was the question asked by a voice inside him, though that isn't to say that he wasn't tormented by a thousand other things in the course of his life, such as mustering the strength to endure close to twenty years at the Customs House, which he endured, all the while keeping his un-interrupted connectedness to the universal, even with nobody understanding what he was saying in *Moby-Dick*, *The Confidence Man*, *Clarel* and so on, yes, he was tormented by humiliations, his existence forgot-ten, his writings unwanted and unread, and not consid-ered a part of what he would eventually indeed become very much a significant part of, and so on, and yes, there was his wife Lizzy and the sisters and daughters and other relatives, and the lost friends, especially the dis-appearance of Hawthorne from his life, and of course the suicide of his son Malcolm, and, early on, the death of his father, and then, during the period I focused on, the death of his mother, and then of course the constant shortage of money, but I don't need to carry on the lit-any of all the thousand items of day to day trauma, for, as I have said, there were a thousand and one things that could and did rack and torment him, and yes, during all that time, even as the Void of Being, which he never ceased to face, rendered him powerless to act, ALL THAT WHILE his connectedness was intact, yes, he was incapable of disconnecting himself, regardless of these thousand and one loads upon his shoulders, and I haven't even mentioned that we know nothing or next to nothing about his life as a Customs Officer, because

I have neglected to say that I was interested only in the Melville who became a Customs Inspector in 1866, since I labored under the impression that what had become knotted up inside him by 1866 constituted what was truly significant in his life, and by then he was well past *Moby-Dick*, by then it had become obvious that he had failed with *Moby-Dick*, something that, seen from my vantage point, seems utterly absurd, how can you fail with *Moby-Dick*?! ... that's like saying the *Iliad* is a failure, or the *Divine Comedy*, and I reflected on this, while still back at the library, as I leafed through the pages of Hershel Parker and Jay Leyda, here was this man with *Moby-Dick* behind him and in front of him the humiliating fact of the reviews and sales figures and a large bottle of brandy, I could envision this Melville, and it became immediately clear that from this point on Melville becomes far more visible, somewhat like Venice in the winter, the way Venice somehow becomes more visible in that misty, rainy, cold season, the devil knows why or how this can be, but that's how it is, and that's how I was with Melville, from the time when he started going to work at the Customs House he becomes understandable for me, of course it's insufferably pompous to make a claim like that or even to think it, because it wasn't that I understood him, but that I *found Melville*, yes, that's more like it, it's not only more modest but more accurate, because the way he started his daily walk toward Broadway, then took a horse-drawn omnibus down to Thirteenth Street, and from there went on by foot on Gansevoort Street to his Shack, or later in life getting off somewhere on the West Side to walk along the Hudson to the Shack, and then back home, the same routes, six days a week, and from all this somehow a picture emerged, of who this Melville was, of how it was with him and with his connectedness to the universal, and the regular daily route and so on, and of course it wasn't at all difficult to tie in Lowry with all of this, since he was always along, and then also Woods, since, after all, as witnessed by the astounding visions I saw in his drawings, he'd arrived effortlessly at connectedness with the universal, and as soon as I imagined Woods on his way to that tavern or to his art supply store, I could see that Woods was already connected, that's how it went, I kept looking for their footprints, that was all, I endeavored to meticulously follow in their footsteps, staying on their tracks as an act of homage, following where they led, and of course in the meantime I was, in a way, actually walking in their company, so that, after a series of these rambles, I myself was present (albeit in my always humble, insufficient way) at the places where each of these geniuses must have expressed his particular genius, the first one /Melville/ by daring to bombard the Rock with questions, monotonously tormenting-to-the-point-of-madness questions of that Emptiness, yes, questioning this Satan-ruled World, the second one /Lowry/ by intuiting upon this same Rock (that is, in fact, via Melville) that he himself possessed to a self-annihilating extent the tremendous courage to pose similar questions, effectively all kinds of similarly excruciating questions, and finally the third

/Woods/ by on the one hand identifying, that is, drawing in his sketchbooks and so drawing attention to this Rock of Manhattan itself, and by possessing on the other hand the courage to reflect in a completely original manner about the very concept of catastrophe and devastation, about how catastrophes—ignoring for now the matter of disasters produced by human evil—and their resulting ruins are not the murderous products of hostile, antihuman forces that we must sweep away and hide and pretend as if they had never happened, but are simply dramatic moments in our ongoing, natural and naturally satanic existence, and in fact, instead of reparations, have been waiting for that clear avowal whereby Woods endowed humankind, and the culture humankind has created, with an incendiary dignity, because he envisioned the reality of a universe present in all of its immediacy, a reality needing no forces of mediation in order to assert its presence, since it is immediate and present, when the earth shakes and rends itself apart, *immediate, just as when* a single hydrogen bomb causes millions to perish, and so Woods declared that all of our attempts to hide this immediacy are false and mendacious, because the universe, with respect to us, operates in its destructive character—manifesting its operations at times through itself, at others through humankind—this is what Woods was saying, and, according to the testimony of his drawings this knowledge was where he arrived during those Manhattan rambles while seated between 3 and 5 p.m. in the quietest nook of his particular tavern, or, when having run out of sketchbooks, he walked to the art supply store on Third Avenue and back, that *people must be told the truth*, and, if you are truly an artist, this is the spirit in which you have to create architecture and poetry and music and science and philosophy, you have to look people in the eye as you tell them the truth about this universe in which we exist, that in fact this universe is in a state of war, there is no peace, the universe means danger, hazard, stress and destruction—nothing is whole and intact, the very notion of an intact whole is a lie—peace and tranquility, permanence and rest are illusions far more dangerous than the truth, for the truth of the universe is indeed danger, hazard, stress and destruction, but denying that, by means of an architecture that is willfully mendacious or just not intelligent enough, as Woods sitting in that tavern demonstrates in his sketchbook, and as his great predecessor Melville had said in his own transfigured manner, denial is tantamount to preventing us from readying ourselves for what has been and what will be, preventing us from confronting our fate, confronting the *actual meaning* of suffering, illusion, and dignity, in other words the actual meaning of the drama that is humanity's lot, oh well, once again I've allowed myself to get a little carried away, I can see how I've given free rein to the pen I'd been using already back there in the library, and still use today, for I'd used a certain pen to start writing, and still use it, this old blue Parker ballpoint I've always used in my notebooks, not finding anything else secure, I have never used and still don't use a laptop for private purposes, much less use the office computers at the library, the running joke about them being that your every single word, all kidding aside, retroactively back to the day you were born is being monitored on them, though here I must make a slight detour, because I must not neglect to mention that, although I'm always mentioning the great democratic community of librarians, I have maintained a profound silence about the alarmingly hierarchic, archaic and dictatorial management of libraries, namely directors, deputy directors, chairpersons and vice-chairpersons, advisors and secretaries, the entire gang of these directors, vice-chairpersons, advisors and secretaries, yes, and the foul hucksters on the boards, those donors and sponsors reeking of untold millions, as well as more sponsors who shuffle around in their board meetings, all of whom in my opinion are of course in bed with the real estate people, they are the ones constantly desecrating libraries by transforming them into lending institutions, and prating about catering to the public—the people, the populace—while in reality, using methods evocative of the most repulsive colonial times, they control all the strings that place libraries at the mercy of everything vulgar, and they have produced a horrid, cold, dismissive and rigid bureaucracy—a bureaucracy that registers even the slightest attack aimed at its essential character, even if it originates in the immediate vicinity, for instance here in the library, in the community of librarians, where, even if you are alone in one of the staff lavatories and happen to mumble to yourself, something about, say, a Permanently Closed Library Palace, anything like that, you are already doomed, you must not even breathe a word about such things or you'll find yourself in a split second out on the street, without any health insurance, in other words, condemned to death, this is America!!!— no wonder that I always wrote only in these notebooks and used a pen, I wasn't crazy enough to risk being kicked out, back then while I still worked at the library I kept cautioning myself, careful, here you are nearing retirement, and you no longer even have a wife, you only have consumer debt, this was what I had to keep in mind, and here I will say no more, I don't want to complain, especially retroactively, because for quite some time after I started filling these notebooks I never got into any trouble at work, and I have now filled twenty-one notebooks, in my very small handwriting, and back at the library no one could have had the least notion of what I was doing, and no one did, not the vaguest idea of what exactly I was doing and thinking and imagining, or at least I had been laboring under that impression, and I performed my duties, that's a fact, which, I must admit, never really taxed me over-much, and actually the brunt of my energies went into constantly pretending that I was busy doing something, fretting constituted the day-to-day gist of my library work as well as picking up a book and putting it down, taking it from here to there, out or in, removing it from a shelf or putting it back, checking it in, checking it out

and so on, well, no wonder I always had enough energy
to turn to my notebooks, surreptitiously at the NYPL
or else at home in the evenings after working hours,
after exiting the 42nd Street building, when I would
either go home and continue to work on my notebook,
or else, if it happened to be the day for it, then—often-
times after a small detour to scurry over to Angelo's
inside Subway Arcade 666, the small Italian shoe repair
shop where I've been going for years because I have to
replace my orthotic inserts frequently—ridiculous to
call them "arch supports," isn't it?—and it's no use tell-
ing them that really it's not flat feet that you have, but
overpronation, people just go ahead and simplify it, and
that's that, so you end up with "arch supports" although
your condition is not fallen arches but overpronation,
oh to hell with it—anyway, if it happened to be the day
for my walk then I would head for the alpha point where
I would set out, and from where it was only a few blocks
to my own apartment, because, as I've already mentioned, the great Herman Melville's residence was near
Park Avenue whereas I, the lower case herman melvill,
lived on the same East Twenty-Sixth Street, but closer
to Second Avenue, I haven't been aware that I was re-
peating myself but now, rereading what I'd written and
revising where needed, because it's quite confusing in
several places, no point denying that, it needs some re-
vision even as I am continuing on, and I still don't know
why I've repeated these localities, when there is another
story to come, one that I wrote down after my time at
the library, well it's all the same now, but the upshot is

that something had happened, something that creates a bit of a sidetrack, though in fact it truly is a sidetrack in the most literal sense of the word, I am not exaggerating here, because this story fits only tangentially into the picture, into this Trinity, and for my own purposes I may call them that in my own notebook, no?, but in a way it does fit in, if only tangentially, and I admit, somewhat arbitrarily, but I may be allowed a small indulgence, no?, after all I am writing this for my own amusement, for that Special Library I have been dreaming of, but I might as well lay my cards on the table and call it *the Special Library that's in its initial planning stages*, these paltry notebooks of mine could only claim a place at the very end of a lowermost shelf, and I am fully aware that when the time arrives, I myself will place them on that shelf ... anyway, what happened was that one evening about a month ago, I no longer recall exactly when, I was helping out at the Information Desk and had remained there a little past regular working hours to put things in order after one of the patrons— and may the lazy jerk's hands fall off—did not bring back the requested reading materials to the shelving cart as he was supposed to do, but left them on his reading desk, left them behind there as, if you'll pardon me, a dog leaves his excrement, and so I had to put things in order, pick up the books and return them, and that's when I noticed three large sheets of notes left behind in one of the books, and as long as I had to remove these since they weren't supposed to remain there, I took a quick peek and then read from beginning to end, after which I must admit that I no longer so keenly detested that person, seeing that he had taken notes about a Hungarian composer quite well known to me, perhaps the notes were meant for a letter or report or an article once he had finished them, I don't know and it doesn't make any difference, but he'd written that he, this note-taker, had gone to visit the building where the Hungarian composer had lived for some time after arriving as a refugee in this country, and this man, the notetaker, had recounted in detail how he had searched for, and found, this building on Cambridge Avenue in Riverdale, up in the heights near Ewen Park, but saw no sign whatsoever on the building, no memorial plaque, nothing to indicate that this world-famous Hungarian composer had once resided there, and I must admit that I am not that familiar with his oeuvre except for his *Concerto for Orchestra*, which I'm sure I've listened to a hundred times, and I must confess that whenever I listened to it alone I always had tears in my eyes, because, at a certain point, in the next to last movement it has a, a, a melody for strings that is so sad, so sad that I just get all choked up every single time although, as I said, aside from this *Concerto for Orchestra* I know nothing else of his, but because of this *Concerto*, I do know his name, and these handwritten notes were about him, perhaps at too great a length, and here I am ashamed to admit I do not know the correct way to write the name, and I no longer have the handwritten notes, which naturally I'd thrown out, but in the composer's name there is an accent over one of the vowels so that it is either Bártok or else Bartók, I'm not sure which, and actually it makes no difference, especially since where I am now I am unable to look it up, the important point is that this Bartok sought refuge in the States at the time of the so-called ominous political changes in Europe, that is, the advance of the Nazis, I think it was in 1941, wasn't it, yes, I remember, it was '41, when he arrived here, in New York, or rather, up in the Bronx, in Riverdale, however, as I later read somewhere, after I became interested in what lay in the background of this *Concerto for Orchestra*, because to tell the truth, I do like to follow up on things, I found out that the sorrowful melody—which, as it happens, I kept listening to right after my wife left me for good again and again all night—might possibly be merely an ironic allusion, the caricature of a tune from a chauvinistic operetta, that is it *probably* (the word was emphatically underlined in the handwritten notes, exactly the way I like to underline everything that I hold to be very important!) was composed amid the complex sorrows of finding one's self so far from one's native land, and moreover by then he was gravely ill, and died right here in Manhattan, which he too detested, not long afterward, but on that house in Riverdale which the notetaker had located at number 3242 Cambridge Avenue, there was no sign whatsoever, no commemoration, not even a dried bunch of flowers, nothing, nothing to state that the world-famous Bartok had resided here for some time near the end of his life, this notetaker noted, though he made no mention of what I found out for myself, that the composer had moved from that building after about two years and led a more or less homeless exile existence in a series of hotels, resorts, sanatoriums and then toward the end, for a few months in 1944–45, lived in a small two-room apartment on West Fifty-Seventh Street, until that final sad hospital ward in the West Side Hospital, all this had not been mentioned by the unknown notetaker, nor the fact that when the composer was buried in a village called Ferncliff ten people all in all attended his funeral, a fact not mentioned by our notetaker most likely because he was more interested in Bartok's concert performances, since it was mostly volumes containing revolting reviews from the American press that he had left behind on his reading room table, instead of—and I will write this down just to be sure, because I can't remember if I'd noted it earlier and today I don't feel like backtracking—instead of bringing them back to where our regulations demand they be returned after use, oh well, some people are just like that, in fact they're all like that, except that they control themselves, otherwise they'd most likely all leave the requested books the way dogs, pardon me again, leave behind their excrement, except they're afraid of a reprimand if they don't bring back the books to the designated shelf, so they return them, at least most of them do, but you'll always find one or two, what shall I call them, negligent types such as my notetaker here, but this one I can forgive, because no matter how we look at it, I owe this sad story to him, it's not just that it is sad, but that it possessed an urgent significance for me, because this man, at the end of his notes, had scribbled several times, without any connection to what went before, or what came after, and in fact after that he wrote nothing else, the rest of the page remaining empty, after

## Bartok in an unmarked building

## Bartok in an unmarked building

and that's all, which gave me the funny feeling that this whole thing looked predestined, or as if he had left the notes for me, since the fate of this Bartok had an uncanny similarity, all right, I am overstating it, let's say it bore a partial resemblance to the great Melville's fate, for both of these men were in fact treated as unknowns, Melville had started to become forgotten *because of Moby-Dick*, until he really and truly was forgotten, essentially up to the time when, about twenty or thirty years after his death, the Melville Revival began to take shape, and with that, gracefully and gradually, they locked him up—and turned the key!—among the Great American Classics, whereas Bartok, *in spite of* the *Concerto for Orchestra*, was properly speaking never really discovered, yet, both cases are, in a word, typical New York stories, come on, you might say now, please spare us such a far-fetched comparison, to which I reply, no, not at all, and in fact all the way through from the very beginning to the end of this story of mine, it was exactly these kinds of "so-called" coincidences that propelled me forward, and therefore I am certain that this little sidetrack about Bartok belongs in my story, for even though there exists a historical marker next to the entrance of 104 East Twenty-Sixth Street, it is so very

*tiny!!!*

that it doesn't take a Lowry in his hyperelevated mood to miss the building, which back then was still unmarked, since the same thing could befall even today's enthusiast looking for this historical marker, because the one placed there, thanks to the evil cunning of its size and placement, is essentially hidden, as if it weren't even there, in other words, and I would like to point out here in my notebook, there is a certain kind of greatness that (and let's say this without any damned romanticizing) posterity simply prefers to keep out of sight, not because of any sloppy frivolousness, but because posterity *never understands them*, the ones on these commemorative plaques, and considered from this angle, Bartok's *Concerto* or Melville's *Moby-Dick*, although both of these works exist, and the world fame of their creators has not been revoked, although I doubt that my colleagues at the library are quite as familiar with the *Concerto* as with *Moby-Dick*, but no matter, these works do exist, and one of them—perhaps—is still read, and the other—perhaps—still performed at times, but in reality both works have continued to be enveloped in total incomprehension, for I am convinced that not only his own contemporaries had not understood

Herman Melville but even now he is not understood, now, when I am writing this, and what's more, he is not even read—all right, put your hand up if you have read *Clarel* all the way through, or even *The Confidence Man*!!!—and never will he be understood, save for one or two specimens such as myself who, even if we do not reach the stage of understanding, at least pay homage, and even though people such as myself and other small fry will always exist, still, is it any help?!, no, it's no help at all!, let's be frank!, because of who are we, of who am I, why, not even my wife could put up with me (and let me repeat: with good reason), anyway, about a month ago this Bartok affair irrupted on me and I'd wanted to write it down quickly so I wouldn't forget it, but then I forgot about it, because so many things happened and keep happening to me day after day, so that a tremendous backlog always remained, and still remains, there's so much left out of these notebooks, things that should have been included, and should be included now, but no matter, let's take things in order, because if my memory serves me well (and it doesn't, it doesn't serve me at all, but never mind), let's say we are back where I am walking the Melville route and all the while am aware that Lowry is present with his Melville-worship as well as Woods with his incendiary visions, both traveling the same path as Melville, and so they arrived at the same place, this is very important now—I have accidentally managed to stumble upon the right words for what I mean to say, because I had by all means intended to write this down with my Parker

57

ballpoint pen, right here, smack in the middle of things, is the very place where I've been heading in this story, or where Melville and Lowry and Woods had been heading in their respective stories, from three different directions, but to the same identical place—though here I must devote a little more attention to Woods's kind of incendiary incitement that you may, for all I care, also call architecture à la Woods, the essentials of which are just as difficult to grasp as they are easy to misrepresent, in speaking or, in my case, writing about his work, captivated as I was by Woods at first sight of his drawings, right at the very first phase of my becoming acquainted with his work, first of all because here was an architect who was not at all interested in whether or not his architectural designs were carried out, in fact I had and still have the definite impression that he never intended for his designs to be actually built, since they were not really architectural designs in the strict sense but rather the drawings of an architect, the graphic expressions of all of his ideas—and here, taking a deep breath, let me write this down again: ideas, not so much about architecture but about thinking itself, about the ways in which we *could* think about architecture, and along with that, about things in general, recognizing the essence of the subject in a way that no one ever had before, so that now we may begin to talk about this essence, or in his case, make drawings about it, and now I should add that I have a hunch that Woods might have suffered corporal punishment at school, his father had been a soldier, or most likely an army engineer, let's polish this picture to make it prettier, for I have reason to believe that already in his childhood Woods had responded to problems exclusively by way of drawings, and that this, sooner or later, was bound to annoy his teachers and perhaps his father as well, at one of the military bases where he spent his childhood they might have asked him, for instance, what was the date of the French Revolution or when was Karl Marx's *Das Kapital* published, or why didn't you finish your homework, and in response he would make a drawing, say, of a Paris where everything was distorted and topsy-turvy compared to the commonly accepted image of Paris, or draw the design of a weapon that self-destructs, that's the sort of thing I'm picturing, his childhood couldn't have been easy, albeit a graphic one, well, no matter, what do I know, I am merely playing with words, it could just as well be that he'd been petted and dandled and patted on the head up till the time when he first entered an architectural office, which happened to be Saarinen's, where he even received a salary for making drawings, who knows, it doesn't matter, what matters is that about a hundred times I have gone through his brochures and monographs and albums and sketches in *Radical Reconstructions*, *OneFiveFour*, *The Storm and the Fall*, *The Ground*, and in *War and Architecture*, and I thought that all right, these are all astounding and they provide a good sense of Woods's way of thinking, but for me his entire life's work somehow pointed in a certain direction, namely toward his project titled *Lower Manhattan*, this was the one that, how shall

I say, not only astounded me, but dumbfounded me, rendered me speechless, the things I had seen in that drawing, and then I started to read those brief and even briefer texts, statements he had made or written about this project and found sentences such as

Why must the history of a place always be understood as the received one? Is the future to be the same, always given?

which right away knocked me out and of course immediately made me think of Melville, the tormented manner of Melville's thinking, the way he would begin something in a chatty tone, and then a few lines down we arrive at the essential, the universal, the Human-Earth connectedness, or whatever, yes only Melville was capable of dazzling me with his train of thought, I'll give you an example that I've looked up, except I can't find it now, to hell with it, well, it makes no difference, but no, wait, here it is, Ahab addressing the severed head of the whale, as Hamlet addressed the skull, here it is,

"Speak, thou vast and venerable head," muttered Ahab, "which, though ungarnished with a beard, yet here and there lookest hoary with mosses; speak, mighty head, and tell us the secret thing that is in thee. Of all divers, thou hast dived the deepest. That head upon which the upper sun now gleams, has moved amid this world's foundations. Where unrecorded names and navies rust, and untold hopes and anchors rot; where in her murderous hold this frigate earth is ballasted with bones of millions of the drowned; there, in that awful water-land, there was thy most familiar home. Thou hast been where bell or diver never went; has slept by many a sailor's side, where sleepless mothers would give their lives to lay them down. Thou saw'st the locked lovers when leaping from their flaming ship; heart to heart they sank beneath the exulting wave; true to each other, when heaven seemed false to them. Thou saw'st the murdered mate when tossed by pirates from the midnight deck; for hours he fell into the deeper midnight of the insatiate maw; and his murderers still sailed on unharmed—while swift lightnings shivered the neighboring ship that would have borne a righteous husband to outstretched, longing arms. O head! thou hast seen enough to split the planets and make an infidel of Abraham, and not one syllable is thine!"

hear that?, and not one syllable is thine!, that is phenomenal, the way he ends up there, well, anyway, the point is that Melville had enchanted, stunned, and dazzled me just as Woods dazzled me with his visions, which I have absorbed, but without ever arriving at full understanding, and I have also discovered why, because in the case of Woods's drawings, just as with Melville's sentences, beyond a certain point there is no further advance to be made toward a full understanding, of course a path of understanding exists but you may advance unobstructed only a certain distance, then comes a point where you can go no further, where you would have to make an acrobatic leap to arrive at perfect understanding, a leap that you are not capable of making, or at least I am not, so you merely abide at this point, and peer in the direction where perfect understanding awaits, peer with deepest awe in that direction, and this gives you the strength to endure your life, to put up with the fact that your life can at best only be a passionate admiration of theirs, but it is precisely this awareness of the distance between you and them, the existence of this distance, that gives importance to your life by giving importance to life itself, well, at this point I could just as well end my notes, since with this, I may have said my say, told everything I'd intended to tell, in any case I won't have anything more grandiloquent than this to say, but I will not stop here, because although this may be what I had meant to set down, I am still not sure if this is all, for there are things I ought to add here, for instance I should explain how I got from constant connectedness to Earth, via the Melville-Woods-Lowry route, to the situation that today, at this very moment, defines my life, so it couldn't hurt to provide a more precise picture of the drawing Woods had made of his Lower Manhattan, because what if the drawing got lost (or, if the ideal will soon enough become the real, when the Permanently Closed Library will have been completed, where nobody would ever be able to look at it again), this drawing that shows, discernible in its outlines, the lower part of Manhattan, but although the outlines can be discerned the island itself is barely recognizable, since Woods has elevated his Manhattan from the usual viewing plane, in other words the New Jersey, Manhattan, and Brooklyn parts are not all in the same plane, for on the East River side Manhattan is plainly *visible* all the way down to its lower depths, Woods having dissected this Manhattan, or more precisely, he has peeled away Manhattan's East River side down to the profoundest depths, so that the entirety of his Manhattan lies atop a vast and *visibly exposed* tremendous mass of bedrock right in the middle of this drawing, the city as we know it is lifted in place up to the heights, leaving the East River and South Brooklyn parts of the drawing as if torn away, or as if dropped down into a tremendous depth, so you see this enormous mass of bedrock that is for Woods the center of everything, and only at the very top of this mass of bedrock can you see the familiar buildings of Manhattan

that are now only approximately—that is to say in fact
not quite—identifiable, certain buildings seem to be
recognizable, and others, such as the twin towers of the
World Trade Center, along with the surrounding buildings, were scaled down by Woods in 1999, so that in
effect he made them disappear, at a time when he
couldn't have had any inkling of what was to happen to
these twin towers two years later on September 11, but
in his 1999 drawing these twin towers fade away as it
were into the gray of the other buildings, barely distin-
guishable, in fact it is impossible to see where they are,
well, no matter, but you are able to see, on the East
River side, the texture of the massive bedrock upon
which Manhattan was built, and seeing this texture is
like glimpsing a crystal's interior geological plates that
have been twisted and contorted by monstrous forces,
where the angles between the various planes form one
enormous convoluted surface—and we may skip the sci-
entific details here, according to which layers of Manhattan schist, Inwood marble and Fordham gneiss once
upon a time had converged here, and that furthermore
right between Midtown and Downtown there exists a
rift, all this stuff though is of no interest here—what
matters is that enormous chunk of bedrock, and you
can see the East River on one side and the Hudson on
the other, but depicted so that the surface of the Hudson is up there at sea level along with New Jersey and
Manhattan, but Woods had drawn in, as an extension
of the bedrock, a dam that retains the Hudson up at its

familiar level while creating with this dam of rock a vast abyss south of approximately where Battery Park meets TriBeCa, leaving the East River looking like the Colorado River in the Grand Canyon, in other words way down there in some bottomless abyss, at a giddying depth compared to the Hudson and Manhattan, but viewed from here, from the Brooklyn side of the East River it is difficult to tell exactly what's going on, because here too Woods installed some sort of dam, one that keeps the water not at the present level but way down there in the depths, that is, he constrained the water down into the chasm that, starting from this side, practically embraces the Rock of Manhattan, with only the Brooklyn Bridge visible way up in the tremendous heights, the rest of the bridges are omitted by Woods in this visionary panorama that also contains one or two other astounding details such as for example his pulling Castle Clinton back to adjoin the Granite of Manhattan, as Woods himself liked to call it, the Granite, but he sinks the castle, too, down into the chasm, and now that I began it, the list could go on, there are other oddities, for example if you turn this work around, I mean view it from the back, you can see that once again he had made use of a photograph, possibly an aerial photo, drawing in some details and drawing over others as well as cutting out parts and then taping in his own additions, thereby creating his own Lower Manhattan, but the point is that when you see this black and white apparition, and it can hardly be called anything else, then after a while you are no longer concerned with the technical details, but with the whole thing, as in, WHAT IS THIS?!, and then you wonder, what if indeed THIS REALLY IS MANHATTAN, because there is something in this drawing that actually is, above all, comforting, and I simply cannot understand those people who scribble complaints about how deeply disturbing they find this Manhattan drawn by Woods, on the contrary, for me this view of Manhattan is comforting, as it were, because it is TRUE, as if this were the REAL MANHATTAN, while the one that we dwell in, today's Manhattan, has been somehow defaced, and this is where I find so helpful Woods's slew of comments, born of vodka and champagne, for they reveal the tremendous speed with which he grasped certain matters, for example, reading that sentence by Le Corbusier he instantly understood what Le Corbusier was talking about, namely, when Le Corbusier once remarked "Manhattan? Oh Manhattan's too small!" and of course people misunderstood him, for New Yorkers believed that he meant oh, the skyscrapers were not tall enough, in other words, even larger, even higher ones needed to be built, whereas Woods immediately saw that that was not at all what Le Corbusier had meant, but, as Woods explained, rather that Manhattan and all its skyscrapers were not big enough when scaled to the *Earth*, upon which they sit, but even this could be misunderstood, so Woods went on to explain, it wasn't that these skyscrapers were too small with regard to their ground plan, but in their scale relative to the Earth, Planet Earth herself,

with which Manhattan was obviously in the closest relationship, since the Granite, as he called the rock upon
which Manhattan was built, manifests itself each and
every day, this rock, the city sits on top of this rock, and
so on, that was Woods for you, he instantly understood
the things that mattered, nor did he lock up within himself what he had understood, but tried to pass it on, for
instance not only in drawings, namely in this drawing
titled *Lower Manhattan*, but also often in spoken comments as well as in written texts, explaining that the
motivation for his drawing (that is, envisioning Manhattan in this manner) was that he had not been satisfied with the Manhattan-image of the inhabitants of
Manhattan, in fact, we might as well say it: he was dissatisfied with the Manhattan of today, which was already there in Lowry's day, and which to an extent had
had its beginnings at the time of Melville's walks, and
the reason he, that is Woods, was dissatisfied was that
he loved, truly loved the real Manhattan, and for this
reason he needed its reality to demonstrate the extent
to which architecture was responsible for our being
sundered not only from Heaven, a rupture that had so
devastated Melville, but from the Earth as well, so that
in fact here in Manhattan we have nothing to do with
the Earth we live on, and therefore have nothing to do
with reality, that is to say everything is covered up, reality is covered up, and an artist's or a philosopher's
task is to demonstrate the plain structure of the relationship that may restore the connectedness between
the Earth and humans, Woods made no mention of the

Heavens, I believe that he did not think too highly of Heaven, perhaps he was downright exasperated by the way humans for thousands of years have been speaking of Heaven, because we are still stuck at that stage, Woods probably thought, and Melville had written about this, he had created *Moby-Dick* and all the rest in this spirit, in the awareness that we have a perverted picture of reality, for according to Melville we have brought about a picture of reality that is mendacious, and stemming from that, a blind society, where people are convinced that they know the nature of the reality they inhabit, whereas they are completely misguided, for they are wrong on both counts, on the one hand they haven't the least notion of what reality is like, and, on the other hand, their conviction that they do know what this reality is like is disastrous, said Woods, as had Melville, too, of course, not to mention Lowry, who had not spoken of this directly, but suffered because of it, because of such falsehood, while in his own intemperate way he had suffered from the truth as well, it broke his heart, and that was how he came to write *Under the Volcano*, with a broken heart, and came to follow in Melville's footsteps, because, let's face it, all three of them were fully aware that *catastrophe* is the natural language of reality, and that catastrophe may originate in nature, but it may also follow from human evil, it makes no difference, and furthermore according to Woods catastrophe is NOT EVEN EVIL, we cannot speak of it as of some evildoer, the way for instance people speak about an earthquake, that at a given location an earthquake of such and such magnitude *killed* a given number of people and devastated this or that city and so on, no, not so, said Woods, who died, as it happened, the night Hurricane Sandy hit New York, but Melville had said the same thing and so did Lowry, there is no such thing as a murderous catastrophe, of course with regard to us yes, granted, but the catastrophe itself cares not a whit about whom it may harm, this is a perilous line of thought if we extend it to human evil, but it still leads in the right direction, Woods believed, as did Melville, for these two, and of course Lowry as well, quite simply refused to take for granted that the point of view from where we consider the universal is self-evident, to put it plainly—which is the only way I can put it, I am being rather hypocritical here, since I am incapable of a more complex wording—in any case the question is, what does one, what does humankind need more: reality or the falsehood we can cover it up with, and they had concluded that falsehood carries a far greater risk, and if that is correct, and we provide, and thereby alarm, people with a true picture of reality, then we must accordingly change our way of life here on Earth, namely, said Melville, as did Woods, and Lowry, drunk as a lord, concurred, we must recognize that catastrophe is permanent and is not aimed at us, catastrophe doesn't give a shit about us, of course it destroys us if we happen to be in its way, but as far as it's concerned, this is not destruction, destruction does not exist, or, to look at this another way, destruction is going on every single moment, and the astounding meaning of Woods's message is that the whole works, the entire workings of the universal is destruction and annihilation, devastation and ruination, how on earth can I say this right, in other words there is no dichotomy at work here, no such thing exists, it is imbecilic to talk about antithetical forces, two opposed sides, a reality describable in terms of mutually complementary concepts, silly to talk about good and evil, *because all is evil, or else nothing is*, for total reality can only be seen as continual destruction, permanent catastrophe, reality is catastrophe, this is what we inhabit, from the most miniscule subatomic particle to the greatest planetary dimensions, everything, do you understand, and again I am not addressing anyone in particular, everything plays the roles of both perpetrator and victim in this drama of inevitable catastrophe, therefore we simply cannot do otherwise than acknowledge this, and deal with the makeup of destruction, for instance the enormous forces that are shaping our Earth at every moment, we must confront the fact of war on Earth, because there is war in the Universe, and here comes Melville again with his brutal notion, that there is all of this and God is nowhere, that benevolent God the creator and judge is nowhere to be found, but instead we have Satan, and nothing but Satan, do you understand?!, by 1851 Melville ALREADY KNEW that *only* that Emptiness of Satan exists, about whom Auden wrote that

/he/ is unspectacular and always human,

And shares our bed and eats at our own
table ...

and I am not quoting this from memory, I had to look it
up, but anyway, the point is that I believe Auden has
really hit the nail on the head, it seems he too is asking
here the same question I am asking, namely, how could
he (Melville) know?, but who would be able to answer
that, am I to say now that Melville knew because he
kept on the move, sailed the oceans?, and the oceans he
had sailed had given him an extraordinary understanding of the Earth?, but I will not make that claim, because for all of this it was essential that he himself be
the one on the move, sail the oceans, and possess this
knowledge, in other words, the knowledge, being on the
move, and the travels by themselves account for nothing and explain nothing, so let us just say, to repeat
myself, he was connected, and all of this connection had
come to him when his spirit was at its freshest, and at
the same time this spirit kept moving, and as he must
have realized THERE IS NO DUALISM IN EXIS-
TENCE, but what does exist, said Melville in *Moby-Dick*,
and *Clarel*, and *Billy Budd*, is man's absurd dignity, as
a result of which the tragedy of man becomes manifest
precisely at the moment, at the sacred moment when
man dares to resist this supreme truth, and at the same
time this resistance is also the key to his dignity by

means of which he seemingly resolves humankind's problem with the universe and the confusion of our ideas about reality, by acknowledging, by proclaiming catastrophe, as the horribly, extraordinarily, fantastically truthful, gorgeous monstrosities seen in the visions of Woods proclaim in the act of collapsing, the catastrophe in the midst of which we dwell, yes, we ourselves dwell in that ceaseless apocalypse that we need not wait for, but need to recognize is already here, and has been present all along, this is what Lowry must have felt as he transported us in *Under the Volcano* into the immediate vicinity, the awesome grandeur and ever-present danger, of the two baleful volcanoes Popocatépetl and Iztaccihuatl, and this is what Melville kept writing about obsessively for his lone self till the end of his life, and Woods in his notebooks, which will indeed find their place on the most splendid and coveted shelf in the Permanently Closed Library, when the time comes for us to build it, and this is no joke, I am not just jabbering, I mean it seriously, as I have already written, and, for my part, especially after these recent weeks, ever since my new tribulations began, my Calvary, if I may call them that, I have actually been considering myself a day laborer, a spadeworker on this Library Palace, or shall I say again, its palace keeper?, now at last I dare to write this down, at least in lower case letters, palace keeper, on whom the whole thing depends, whether it stands or falls, and I must confess I have shivers running up my spine at this thought, *palace keeper*, and I quickly cover the words with my palm, as if someone from the library could catch a glimpse, even though I am no longer at the library, so no one will see this, in part because I always write with my back turned to them, and then hide away what I write, I won't say where, and so, this way, for the time being, there has been no indication that anyone has noticed, no one here pays any attention to what I do or don't do, as long as I abide by the rules and regulations, I am just a short-statured hunchback librarian with plantar fasciitis, that's all, and I am not merely talking off the top of my head, because I am really and truly short-statured and have a hump, true, it's only a slight one, but it is real, and as I have already stated a few times, I've had over-pronation ever since my childhood, and the only pecu-liarity of mine worth mentioning is my name, so who would take an interest in me, no one, although I ought to mention here that about two weeks ago, on a Wednes-day, when in the evening I'd dared for the first time to write Keeper of the Palace with capital letters, I ran into my department head in the corridor leading to the staff bathroom, yes, the department head herself, and I must say that when I greeted her and she did not re-spond, which wasn't unusual or rude, since usually she didn't, except in the morning and at the end of the day, so it wasn't that, but just the way she looked at me that made my heart freeze, because it flashed through me that *she knew*, I am serious, there I stood in the bath-room afterward, my pants unbuttoned, and even though

I really had to pee, I couldn't, not a drop, because that glare from my department chief made me so upset, and over forty-one years I've had quite a few department heads, but this one, she was the most dangerous of all, because when she joined the staff the first thing she made clear was that we were all on her turf, this was her territory, she was the sovereign ruler, everything here had to have her approval, this was a work zone, as she liked to say, and in this work zone we must maintain a military order, this is a *librrrary*, she said leaning slightly forward, her hoarse alto warning the workers in her department, and this *librrrary* of hers made me sweat bullets right from her first day, it was as if she had said, this is West Pointtttt, all the while with a hint of a smile, because she always had that hint of a smile, even as she tossed the most murderous comments at us either in emails, which was how she usually communicated with her underlings, or else face to face, but we avoided actual encounters as much as possible, and in fact she did too, and it was so obvious that she despised all of us, this most stylish dresser, yes, one might say she had luxurious tastes, exorbitantly expensive shoes, elegant ensembles, scarves, hats, handbags, as if she were not just the head of a department but straight from the director's office, and by her style of dressing, and the way she never availed herself of the side entrance on Forty-Second Street that we all used, but rather chose the director's entrance and exit, she had emphatically let it be known that she was not one of us, she belonged to a higher caste, as proclaimed by the little ribbon on her Prada shoes from Madison Avenue, her scarf from Kleinfeld Bridal, her dress and hat from Chloe, yes, she was of a caste, perhaps not the highest, but high enough so that we couldn't comprehend what it really was and where it fit in, which was why email was her favorite mode of communication and not face-to-face contact, and, when obliged to speak to you in person, she made it clear that she begrudged it, thought it a waste of time, it hurt her to waste time, well, no matter, when at last I was done peeing, there I was, creeping, no, crawling, on my way back from the bath-room, hugging the wall, hoping not to run into her yet again, because it really seemed that she suspected something, perhaps nothing definite, merely that I was someone who might be capable of cooking up something against her, whereas I, well, other than the Spadework conducted in my fantasies, what else could I have been cooking up, at most some water for tea in the staff room microwave behind the loan services desk, but I con-cluded that in any case I had to be more careful, so I began to be more careful, I changed the style of my re-plies to office emails, my tone if anything became more respectful, I endeavored to be more thorough, or, if not more respectful, then more painstaking than previ-ously, but the fear was in me now, I had been found out, she was on to me, she was already aware of something that I could never again conceal, even though at the time there'd of course been no mention of my great dis-covery, since I only revealed that this past week, when once again I was on my way from point alpha to point omega, and this time I had penetrated quite deep, down to the Financial District, and once I was there—after all I was quite certain that Melville himself had taken various routes at various times, when he, too, penetrated farther downtown—I turned off in the direction of Bowling Green, and I'm not going to say I've never seen it before, because I've been to Bowling Green enough times in my long life, but somehow until now I had always seen it with unseeing eyes, more as if I were aware that it was there, without actually seeing it, because I had never looked up, but this time I did, I walked on Church Street past the intersection with Worth Street, and suddenly I found myself at Thomas Street, an insignificant little street, at least this part of it, actually more like a narrow alley, the site of one of the tech buildings of AT&T, when I abruptly found myself looking up at it, and possibly it was the first time I saw it with fresh eyes, in any case, for certain this was the first time I beheld it like this, and I suddenly saw the kind of building it was, at first only its rough surface, then its color, and then my eyes scanned up along the sheer walls until reaching the air vents, and past these all the way to the top, where there were a few additional symmetrical air vents, and nothing more, my eyes ran up and down this façade, over this immaculate surface, which was practically uninterrupted by anything, meaning not a window, not a casement, simply nothing, there was only the wall, the bare wall, so that the upward sweep of my gaze was literally unhindered, and at first I really refused to believe my eyes, was I actually seeing what I was seeing, which was *the Ideal itself here on Earth*, as I rapidly walked around it, and then I paced back to Worth Street, then turned on Lafayette Place to the other side, from there back onto Thomas, and there I stood once again, where I had stood just before, and the blood froze in my veins, for the building I am talking about, one that is quite well-known, and not only locals, but even tourists frequently pass that way, and about which all I had heard was that it had been built by the telecommunications company AT&T for its own use back in the 1970s for some technological purpose, this building was the Ideal Block itself, completely without windows and doors on all four sides nearly, four smooth concrete walls tinted a brown color, though to be more precise, there were two embrasures sunk into the three gigantic columns of the façade facing Worth and Thomas Street but without spoiling the effect, yes, here someone by means of four gigantic, clean and unornamented wall surfaces had created just what I had dreamt for myself (or more accurately, for all humankind) or to curb my wild enthusiasm and be less grandiose, even though, truth to tell, I don't want to curb myself, well, then I will merely say, for Manhattan, because this was the Place, where all we have to do is just bring books in, and stack them up, all in good order, a simple library system will do just fine, and then at the end run one's fingers over their spines on the last shelf, give it one final look, and then leave, and wall everything in, wall it in, and finally at the very end wall up that diminutive entrance, the way they'd walled it up everywhere else, flawlessly, these genius architects and designers, when they had raised this building into breakneck heights on that site here between Church Street and Worth Street, and now, at this point I better take a big breath and reveal at last what this is all about, namely, that I have found it, the site of the Library, the Library that, shall I put it this way?, will become established under the absolute dominion of the Catastrophe-Constant, abbreviated C-Constant, the Library in front of which the palace guards will tend to security duties, I can see it all with my eyes closed, just as I have seen it in reality in front of my open eyes exactly where and how I'd imagined it, but previously it had lived only in my imagination, I had never thought that it *already existed*, that all my life I have roamed about in its vicinity, what's more, and during recent times on my Melville rambles I was practically at its base, obviously I must have passed by it more than once, though that was really hard to believe, and it was brown in color, precisely that shade of dark brown I love best, a shade that happened to be most appropriate for this purpose, and there was nothing about it that might have been objectionable, nothing to imply some kind of trick was being played here, that it might actually possess cleverly concealed windows and doors, no, not at all, there were no doors, no windows here, except for one minor—and I very much want to emphasize—*temporary* mistake, a negligible little entrance on Thomas Street, very cool, placed there, and, I almost said, accidentally left behind there, a few steps and two adjacent revolving doors with glass panels, quite obviously kept locked to the public except for one or two AT&T employees, and I immediately decided these doors could be made to disappear quite easily, and not only these humble, glassed, extremely cool twin doors but naturally also the steps leading to them, in order to eradicate even the slightest notion of an entrance to this exquisite building once we were done with our task, I was already thinking in the plural, although it had to be kept in the singular, because as I looked around to check if anyone had noticed that I happened to be nosing about at this particular spot of all places, it flashed on me that I must leave at once to avoid calling someone's attention to this building's existence and any possible interest it might have for whatever reason to anyone at any time, and I was especially fearful of the Japanese tourist girls, one dreads them because they always accidentally manage to be in places where they shouldn't be, as if this were just the right spot to have some mishap with their cameras, or these days more likely it's their iPhones or iPads, the devil knows what they're using now, very often it's exactly in such places where they sprain an ankle or find a run in their stocking, or whatever, but I didn't see a trace of Japanese girls, so before I came across one, I quickly made off, quickly out to Church, took a left on Worth, and I was gone, I was in such a hurry that soon I had to stop to catch my breath, which I did when I was at a safe enough distance, but still I didn't dare to look back, because to tell the truth I wanted to conceal even my glances, and although the sentences that broke loose inside me like ice floes in a spring thaw were still in the plural, I ascertained that I was alone, by which I mean that unless I go crazy, and there is no reason why I should, then I must admit that all my cogitations about my library colleagues (that we all belong together) from here on no longer applied to the situation regarding what I had until now been referring to as my dream, yes, from here on it would be different, I would be on my own, by myself, I concluded, having to admit that if what I have been calling the Permanently Closed Library was to be realized, as it must be, then the work, no matter how unrealistic this sounds, would have to be accomplished by myself alone, that is, *I alone, all by my lonesome self, must accomplish the transfer of all the books from the New York Public Library to their new location,* all 53 million of them, and only the devil however knows *exactly* how many had to be brought here, to this magnificent Block, so that I quickly went home, sat down in my easy chair in the nearly empty apartment, oh, I forgot to mention that early in the previous week, on a Monday to be precise, when everything is always so depressing anyway—yes, here comes another week, everyone is grumpy and moping, in a bad mood, full of complaints, and so on and so forth—well, last Monday on account of my allegedly lax work ethic my salary was cut, which right away made me realize I wouldn't be able to make the monthly payments on my credit cards, so that as of last Monday I already became subject, so to speak, to foreclosure, but, to be frank, I didn't care, and now I really don't, I don't even know what happened to my apartment, at any rate on that Monday when I went home, for I went home right away, as soon as I had the notice in my hand regarding my salary reduction, I was already thinking that they could take my TV, the bed, the furniture, the kitchen sink, take all of it, whatever they want, I don't need anything, because I had such a formidable task ahead of me that it made all such personal aggravations seem trivial, and from that moment on a profound serenity took hold of me, and for the next two days, making use of my own personal laptop, because I didn't go to work at the Public Library, and I didn't give a shit—if they cut my salary then I'd cut my working hours—and I launched a search, and by the way that was one of the charges against me, that I'd conducted my own private research during working hours, and let me write it down here, I was fully aware that they knew!, anyway, it doesn't matter, for two days I did nothing else but research, first of all I had to find out all there was to know about the building itself, and I did, I learned everything I needed to know, actually I just needed to know the architect's name, and that was easy enough, his name was Warnecke, John Carl Warnecke, a well-known architect in his day, I haven't the least idea what Woods thought of him, although I don't believe that a Lebbeus Woods would have thought much of a Warnecke, or of contextual architecture as such, not to mention the close relationship between Warnecke and the Kennedys, in my opinion Woods was the kind of architect who probably

was not so crazy about architecture itself, but no matter, here was this Warnecke, and the volume got turned
all the way up in my head now, the tension was at its
highest, if I may put it that way, and by that I mean my
head nearly split apart, I was cogitating at such inten-
sity, soaking up all the information, soaking up all that
mattered for me about Warnecke as well, about when
he began the project and what kind of materials he
used, and how the construction progressed, where he
obtained the precast concrete panels for the walls and
the flame-treated textured granite faces, *and there you
are*, this too was granite—I am just pointing that out in
passing!!!—making up the surface of the facades, I
learned the dimensions, and how the foundations were
laid out, this was especially significant, and I found everything in order, to the extent that I was capable of
understanding the technical details, and next I hunted
up the distances between ventilating units, and how the
elevators operated and on how many floors, and of
course I had to find out, and I did, what AT&T and
Verizon were using the building for these days, but this
didn't bother me, I could make no sense of 4ESS elec-
tronic switching systems, CLEC-service, not to mention
CLLI codes, none of that was of interest to me, what
matters is—yes, away with all that crap, who needs it—
all I need are shelves, and, because the individual floors
were built to bear unusual loads, I also read somewhere
that they were designed to bear up to 200 to 300 pounds
per square foot, that is tremendous, I thought, after I
calculated the approximate weight of books stored on

approximately this much square footage, and realized that the books would be featherweight compared to such huge load-bearing capacities, so all this was superbly suitable, although I found slightly disturbing the occasional comment on my laptop screen about why this structure was built so securely, and in this regard I encountered some obfuscation, a reference to some database, just a passing mention, that's all, ah well, I thought ... a mystery, there will be plenty of those here, we'll solve that somehow, and so I gave up trying to decode this technical language that I so often find rather forbidding, the description of what lay inside the building, for my purposes all that was not of the least interest, nothing to research there, I really had no need for anything other than to find out what it looked like on the inside, and I did find that out, and I checked it out, to make sure that it was suitable for my special purpose, and when I found out that 33 Thomas was technically a self-sufficient entity then I became convinced that the building would not only be suitable but downright platonically ideal, it is that suitable, really, to convert from some lousy telecommunications facility into the world's first *actual and closed, yes, by God, permanently closed* megalibrary, I know, I am perfectly aware that of course for me alone to accomplish this will not be a simple task, but I have reached a point where, since I possess extraordinary powers of concentration, capable of shutting out everything, absolutely everything in my environment, so that nothing obstructs me from paying attention to what needs my attention, I did not become anxious, nor am I anxious today, because I know this city, I know its flimsy, vulnerable systems, I am fully aware of how easily the so-called security apparatus of this enormous entity that is New York City may be disrupted, that is, utilized, just as I am well aware of what I can count on in my immediate environment and in my given situation, until I reach the stage of taking action, after all I had clearly perceived that all the machinations behind my salary cut were not the result of some sudden, quick decision, oh not at all, obviously they had been keeping me under surveillance for quite some time, ever since that time when I had noticed, on the way to the bathroom, that expression on the face of my department head that told me she knew that I knew that she knew, as they say, which meant that they didn't just all of a sudden, bang-bang, sit down to compose that notice about my salary cut, oh no, the insidious plot had been hatched step by step, I am certain of that, and actually I should have been aware of this all along, except that I wasn't vigilant enough, they'd been observing me well before that scene on the way to the bathroom, they might have found out, if from no other source than my dearly beloved colleagues, that during those lulls when there was absolutely nothing to do, nothing to be taken from here to there, I was always engrossed in my notebooks, and in any case I am convinced that they were watching me, and keeping me under observation, but it must have taken weeks, I am sure of that, until they decided on my pay cut, and I have forgotten to mention this till now, that along with the notice about my salary reduction came a *warning* as well, yes, that too, I received from my department head, a warning that I should pay greater attention to my professional duties, and during working hours no private business whatsoever was permitted, that was how she phrased it, my department head, *private business*, I would have liked to see the expression on her face had she known what my private business was all about, but she didn't have the least idea, nor will she ever, until I have accomplished my task, and furthermore, I have also forgotten to mention that afterward, on the following day, but we might as well just say last Monday, I received an email—naturally, once again an email!—another edict letting me know that my work hours have been curtailed, due to a certain problem with the state of my health, what problem was she referring to, I wondered, not suspecting what was about to happen since I have no serious health problems, never have had any, mine has always been an iron constitution, I thought, come on, why should it be otherwise now, the note said it was of course by mutual agreement, when I was suddenly sent home, that too on a Monday, on that same Monday, though by then I had lost all sense of time, or rather never before had I felt so clearly that I no longer had to *unconditionally* subject myself to the conventional system of dividing into hours and days and weeks and months and years something that does not in the least transpire along the lines of this system, and the email that Monday ended by recommending that I should without delay seek treatment for my condition at a suitable clinic, which I did not do, of course I didn't give a shit about any of that, I simply went home that Monday, and by now it seems as if all this had happened yesterday, it doesn't matter, it was really all the same to me by then, let them scribble whatever they want, back home in my easy chair it was nice and quiet as I began to think things over, planning how I should go about all this, and so I decided to suspend the Melville rambles for the time being, or maybe for good, I was not yet quite sure, without having adjusted the route, given that after some years Melville was no longer going to work by the Hudson but rather to an East River pier much closer to where he was living, yet I seemed to have reached the end of these rambles, for after all—thanks to Melville, to Lowry, and to Woods—at long last all was clear, they had helped me to assemble in my head the code—I am slightly overstating this—of all that they (not only through their works and their statements and their lives but through each and every breath) had meant to let us know, that is, what was what, the inside story, that is, the situation in the universe, and that accordingly we had to urgently rearrange our lives, you must change your life, I said to myself, partially echoing Rilke's famous dictum, except that I understood it as *de*-range, wind down, resign, and it was no accident that I used the verb "de-range" instead of rearrange, for I had in mind something entirely different from what Rilke in his day had been thinking,

I told myself, derange, which in my case meant resign, because I no longer had the least interest in my own life, it no longer interests me today nor will it ever again, I just have a task, I no longer have a life, only a task, regarding which it goes without saying I had plenty to ruminate about very carefully, especially on that Monday evening, namely how to proceed, but do not take this to mean, and once again I am not address-ing anyone in particular, I just can't say this otherwise, do not take this to mean that there I sat agonizing in my easy chair, brooding—nope, none of that crap, I knew right away what the first step was, and the sec-ond, and the third, except that there were about ten thousand steps, and they all had to be considered, and had to be gone over thoroughly, and therefore I set about doing that, for each of these steps was enormously important, and began with Melville, and reviewing the things I believed important—such as the time Melville took his grandchild to Madison Square, to the play-ground, but upon his return home, when the alarmed family inquired what happened to the child, he could not answer, he had simply forgotten about the child, left her behind in Madison Square—I once more went over the twelve years he spent at Arrowhead, and recalled how in his old age, when he was already utterly forgot-ten, he tended the roses in the backyard of his house at number 104, and also the incident when, taking one of his walks, he supposedly stopped at the Hotel Gan-sevoort, or someplace like that, he had had to face the fact that the young waitress did not have the slightest idea of who Gansevoort had been, this name had no meaning for her whatsoever, and finally once more I went over Melville's handwriting, which was unreadable, and not only unreadable, but, let's face it, *faulty* as well, and in addition he frequently wrote on little slips of paper that he pinned, or laid out somewhere, and from early on he had his sisters helping copy those, but later chiefly relied upon his wife Lizzy, for the sisters and especially Lizzy all had legible handwriting, meaning they produced the fair copy submitted to publishers, however no one, not the sisters and not even Lizzy had permission to add *any kind* of punctuation in the course of copying and making legible Melville's manuscripts, punctuation marks were forbidden for anyone else in the Melville household, only he, Melville, was allowed to insert them, and insert them he did, just before the manuscript was sent to the publisher, that is to the printer, and then after a while, nowhere, because Melville had simply lost the desire to publish, and in addition I also recollected that insane story of Lowry arriving in New York in 1934, and being asked by the customs officer—not Melville the customs officer, but a real one—Mr. Lowry, what have you in your suitcase, Lowry just shrugged and said he didn't recall, why don't we take a look, so the customs man opened the sizable suitcase and all it contained was a single rugby shoe, not a pair, just *one*, plus a worn copy of *Moby-Dick*, and I tried to reimagine once more what it must have been like just before departure, there was Lowry somewhere in Europe, opening that big old suitcase, eyeing his be-

longings, picking up a shirt, and saying, shirt?, don't
need that, toss it aside, jacket?, not needed, toss it aside,
toothbrush and toothpaste?, not needed, toss them
aside, and so on, chucking aside everything of no interest, until he had the rugby shoe and that copy of *Moby-
Dick* in his hands, gave them some thought, dropped
them in the suitcase, shut it, boarded the ship, sailed to
America, why on earth do you find this so surprising,
officer, he asked shaking his head, seeing the rather
bewildered expression of the customs officer, then probably added, uh, come on, what's so unusual about this
that it needs an explanation, this is what I brought with
me, that's all, obviously because this is what I needed,
and Lowry let the customs official wonder in amaze-
ment at this European traveler with nothing but
a rugby shoe and a cheap edition of *Moby-Dick*, and
then finally I reviewed Woods as well, for I had located
his widow Aleksandra Wagner, requested a meeting and
was granted one, all the way downtown in the Financial
District, and from her I learned (in addition to the
names of the taverns, the art supply store and the
sketchbooks and the Dunhills, the vodka and champagne) that for Woods the difference between *size* and
*scale* came to acquire a vital significance, and that the
one thing he couldn't stand was the type of person who
spoke very fast, he detested fast-talking people, to the
extent that he even included them in his famous Resistance Checklist, which I tried to recall, to review that
also once more, and from memory wrote down some of
it as follows,

Resist whatever seems inevitable.

Resist people who seem invincible.

Resist any idea that contains the word *algorithm*.

Resist the impulse to draw blob-like shapes.

Resist the desire to travel to Paris in the spring.

Resist the desire to move to Los Angeles, anytime.

Resist the idea that architecture is a building.

Resist the idea that architecture can save the world.

Resist taking the path of least resistance.

Resist the temptation to talk fast.

finding this not enough, I picked up an earlier notebook, and looked it up, coming across the following, such as

Resist the embrace of those who have lost.

Resist taking the path of least resistance.

Resist the influence of the appealing.

Resist the growing conviction that They are right.

Resist believing that the result is the most important thing.

Resist the claim that history is concerned with the past.

Resist the judgment that it is only valid if you can do it again.

Resist the desire to move to a different city.

Resist that feeling of utter exhaustion.

Resist hoping that next year will be better.

Resist accepting your fate.

Resist people who tell you to resist.

Resist the panicky feeling that you are alone.

and here I admit that all this almost blew my mind, and I may as well add that currently I'm in the appropriate place for that, and, as I said to myself, oh yes, that's how it was, exactly like that, these three students of catastrophe have drummed it into us, if we could only grasp it, catastrophe is our natural medium, and therefore everyone must find a suitable task, such as I myself have found, a fitting response in acknowledgment of

the actual makeup of reality, constructing and walling
in a vast Library, one that, and I cannot reiterate this
enough, we shall only be able to admire *from a distance*,
yes, this resonated in my head for quite some time, so
that by now it was, say, Wednesday afternoon, and I
was still sitting there in that easy chair, at least that's
what it seems like, but of course it was still that same
Monday, if you know what I mean, although as far as
I'm concerned you can call it Thursday, my memory
was never all that good, but when they came to get me,
my department head was there as well, I have no idea
why, though it seemed she was on the brink of crying,
on account of betraying me and having me taken away,
just because the bitch found out what I may have been
planning, although she couldn't possibly have known
exactly what, at most she might have suspected that
I'd been up to something, but she couldn't have known
exactly what, it's simply out of the question, how could
she have known—even as she was hypocritically pat-
ting my hand while the 911 crew escorted me from my
easy chair out to the ambulance, its lights flashing—
that she was up against a person who had his own idea
about things, things he's not willing to write down in
this notebook, things he won't even whisper about, for
it is only a matter of time before I start my task, under no circumstances will I give it up, I have worked
out the proper methods for doing everything, including
how I will have AT&T empty that building—get it?!—I
did not write how I will have the AT&T building emp-
tied, I wrote how I will *have* AT&T empty the building,

just as I have precise plans on how to have everything transported from the NYPL under cover of darkness, and I wonder if anyone's paying attention to the precise wording here, the *causative* construction, but no matter, perhaps I can reveal this much, they'll never catch me anyway, I haven't the least doubt that I will get out of this place, just as back then Lowry had managed, for it was not Plantagenet who'd been here, Plantagenet had never been an inmate of the psychiatric wing of Bellevue Hospital, he received accommodations exclusively on the pages of *Lunar Caustic*, whereas Lowry, he most certainly spent time at Bellevue, and even if he was lying when he later claimed that he had checked in voluntarily, for the purpose of collecting material, Lowry did manage to get out in the end, as I said about ten days was sufficient for him, and he was out but that doesn't matter, the point is that if an alcoholic wreck such as Lowry could get out, then I don't see why it would cost me much more effort, and anyway, never mind, somehow in the not too distant future I too will make my getaway, scurry out like a mouse, as it were, I don't know if you've noticed, and again of course I'm not thinking of anyone in particular, it's just a manner of speaking, noticed that I said scurry out *like a mouse*, that's what I said, and if you could see me now you'd notice a *tiny* little wink, well, it doesn't matter, if you don't get it you don't get it, it's all the same to me, the point is, when they stop pumping me full of all kinds of injections, and I manage to muster a bit of energy, for all these so-called treatments that—and, I can write

this down here, just for the record—are totally unnec-
essary, they do not deter me at all but only make me
weaker, that's all they do, I am constantly sleepy, just
so filthily doped up, no denying it, but this will end
and I will get stronger, or shall I say I will regain my
former energetic self, I will even make use of my department head's visits, I have forgotten to mention that
she still visits me!!!, brings me so many treats, snacks
and beverages, and even flowers!!!, for me!!!, and sits by
my bedside and gazes at me as if she wanted to caress
my hand, but I am vigilant, and snatch my hand away
when hers starts creeping my way, but she won't give
up, she keeps trying again and again, it blows my mind,
indeed now I am in the right place for that, and she is
acting exactly as if she were devoted to me, whereas
it is totally obvious that even now, by means of such
underhanded methods, she's dying to learn more about
what she has already sensed but about which she needs
to find out more, so she shows up every second or third
afternoon, during visiting hours, carrying such a verrry
elegant little basket full of fruit and juices and flowers, and from time to time she brings my preordered
"orthotic inserts" from Angelo's, which are, alas, much
needed on account of my constant use of slippers here,
but never mind, I won't waste any more words on it,
one thing is certain, I am on the alert and will never
let slip a word about what is about to happen, forget
style now, the point is that I will get going on my task,
she cannot prevent my doing that, all these visits and
little baskets and *how badly they miss me at the library*

are no use, oh yes, I can very well imagine *how badly* they miss me, meanwhile never a word about how she happened to be the one who had me brought here by 911, and not quite accidentally here, since this is in my neighborhood, so that, just between ourselves, it would have been easier to tuck her hand under my arm and walk me over here, but it is kind of hair-raising, no?!, that she had me brought to the very place where Lowry stayed, except that I am neither an alcoholic nor weak in the head, it's all in vain, they can treat me as if I'd had a breakdown, they can say anything, this notebook, with this final annotation in it, will be my witness that a dream has been realized, for I am not giving up, I will write it down yet one more time: the PERMANENTLY CLOSED LIBRARY exists, for it must exist, and after having found it inside the circumference of the three most prominent locations for Melville, Lowry and Woods, this notebook of mine, the twenty-something-eth, I don't even know how many I have filled by now, but no matter, this one, here, will be the last thing I will place there at the end, when the great work is finished, and the miraculous operation of walling up the entrance will begin at the entrance of 33 Thomas Street, because it must be brought into existence, it must be finished, someone has to bring it into existence and complete it, for the trail that has been blazed by Melville, Lowry and Woods leads here and here alone, in order that at a time of permanent catastrophe, as a defensive fortress, or let's say as a memorial, at least one Ideal Library Dedicated to Knowledge will exist on Earth, or more precisely a library dedicated to *all that refers* to Knowledge, because someone had dreamed it, someone not myself, for I am merely a day laborer, a spadeworker on this dream, a herman melvill, a librarian from the lending desk, and, yes, currently an inmate at Bellevue, but at the same time—may I say this?—actually a Keeper of the Palace.